RIVERDALE

THE DAY BEFORE

RIVERDALE

THE DAY BEFORE

A prequel novel by Micol Ostow

SCHOLASTIC INC.

Scholastic Children's Books,
Euston House, 24 Eversholt Street,
London NW1 1DB, UK
A division of Scholastic Ltd

London ~ New York ~ Toronto ~ Sydney ~ Auckland
Mexico City ~ New Delhi ~ Hong Kong
First published in the US by Scholastic Inc., 2019
This edition published in the UK by Scholastic Ltd, 2019

Book design by Heather Daugherty
Copyright © 2019 Archie Publications
All rights reserved
ISBN 978 1338 28944 2

Printed and bound in the UK by CPI Ltd, Croydon, CR0 4YY

2 4 6 8 10 9 7 5 3 1

PROLOGUE

JUGHEAD

Riverdale is known as "the town with pep!" But stick around here long enough, and you start to realize just how many of those pasted-on smiles are really only covering up a Narnia-sized closet full of skeletons. Sure, every small town has its secrets. But even those of us who've grown up here, who've lived our whole lives in Riverdale, are shocked at what's being pulled from Pandora's box.

Trust me, I should know. Lately, I've realized that everyone I care about is tangled up in one Lynch-esque melodrama after another.

Riverdale's also a town of Rockwellian traditions: the midnight pancake banquet in late winter, frost lacing the Town Hall windows and vapor curling from our mouths when—if—we dare to step outside. Or the Riverdale High School Homecoming weekend, a network-TV-ready worship of the apex of Americana: football, dancing, and small-town pride.

But my personal favorite—really, the only one that's ever meant anything to me—has to be the annual July 4th Summerfest Carnival. Typically, Betty, Archie, and I would hit up the carnival together, stuffing our faces with hot dogs and cotton candy and testing our skills at the dunk tank (Betty always did have the best arm). By evening, Archie and I would hit the road to check out the Centerville fireworks, Betty hanging back to catch Riverdale's display with her sister, Polly (she never minded being the third wheel with Polly and—more recently—Polly's attached-at-the-hip boyfriend, Jason). The Summerfest is just what we do. What we've always done. Archie and I started going before we were even walking, thanks to our parents. Betty started tagging along around first grade. And it's been a thing ever since.

Or, I should say: It was a thing.

Because this summer, everything's different. Betty's off in LA, honing her writing skills with an internship at Hello Giggles. (Not to mention, Polly and Jason had an epic, scorched-earth breakup on par with The War of the Roses.) Archie's been busy working construction for his dad . . .

Honestly, I haven't seen much of him lately. I don't know. Don't ask me about it.

As for me? So far, so summer-usual. I'm working nights at the Twilight Drive-In, trying to earn some cash, stay out of the house, and stay out of my dad's way, too . . .

Staying out of the way is what I do best, taking things in from a distance, and writing them down.

Meanwhile, while none of us knew it at the time, off in New York City, a young socialite named Veronica Lodge was carelessly living out her own personal episode of Gossip Girl, *courtesy of her daddy, one Hiram Lodge's bottomless bank account. Veronica's parents had history with Riverdale, but, hey—that had nothing to do with us.*

Well, that's what we thought, anyway.

The butterfly effect suggests that small causes can have unpredictable—and catastrophic—effects. One action. A cascade of ripples. An outcome no one can predict.

That was us that summer. Archie, Betty, Veronica, and me. It was July 3. The holiday stretched out in front of us like a broken promise. We were separate but intertwined in ways we'd never see coming. Small, stupid butterflies, blindly flapping our wings.

PART I: MORNING

From: DDoiley1@AdventureScouts.net
To: [list: All_Scout_Mailing]
Re: Overnight supplies list

To all Riverdale Adventure Scouts:

Hopefully, you're all prepared for tonight's campout. (You wouldn't be my Scouts if you didn't know to prepare for any and all eventualities!) Please see below for a comprehensive list of supplies:

    *external frame backpack

    *tent

(Don't forget stakes, guylines, and your tent footprint! The ground in Sweetwater Woods can get very muddy.

    *sleeping bag (with optional liner)

    *multitool—*no pocketknives* per Scoutmaster's regulations

    *flashlights (and extra batteries)

    *swimsuit

    *waterproof sandals

    *long underwear, pajamas, and socks for sleeping

    *water bottle

    *energy bars or other small snacks

    *sunscreen

    *lip balm

    *toilet paper

*insect repellent

*toothbrush/toiletry kit as needed

I'll bring the **first aid kit.** You may also want to bring a **camera,** your **binoculars,** and the attached **field guide to Sweetwater Woods** (though you should all be familiar with its topography by now).

You should also be prepared for two vigorous hikes: first, to camp this evening, and tomorrow morning at sunrise. Badges will be distributed to those who can correctly identify select species of flora and fauna on either or both hikes.

I look forward to spending the holiday with such capable Scouts-in-Training as yourselves! Let me know if you have any questions.

Sincerely,
Scoutmaster Dilton

Cheryl:

Jay-Jay, FYI, Daddy's looking for u. Warpath.
Lay low, but you'll have to face music eventually.

Jason:

Thanks, I'm on it. See you soon?

Cheryl:

En route. Just dodged Daddy Dearest obvi. xo

CHAPTER ONE

BETTY

Dear Diary:

I can't believe it's the Fourth of July already! It's super weird to be celebrating it here in LA, away from Polly and Archie and Jughead. I can't remember the last time we missed the Riverdale Summerfest. I guess it must have been that one summer, when Archie broke his arm building a tree house with Jughead, and we stayed indoors all day reading comics and eating red-white-and-blue ice pops. Everyone's tongues turned bright purple, and Juggie ate three ice pops for every one of Archie's and mine. But that was years ago.

I miss Riverdale, of course, and my friends. But LA is AMAZING. Aunt Gertrude's house may smell a little funny (whatever it is, I seriously think the odor's been absorbed into the walls. It's like a weird mix of garlic and old-lady soap), but she lives right on the edge of Runyon Canyon. So every day I get to hike Runyon Canyon before work. The view is insane. It's exhilarating. There's nothing like it in Riverdale.

The weather's amazing, the barista at Blackwood Coffee knows my order by now (pour over, milk, and two sugars) . . . Oh, and one other thing . . .

Yeah, I miss Polly. But being away from Mom for the first time?

Um, it's not bad.

Obviously, I love her and I know she loves me, but she's so controlling. For once, I feel like I have some independence. And it doesn't suck.

I love working at *Hello Giggles*, too. Even if I have yet to win over my boss, aka the features editor, Rebecca Santos. I don't know if she thinks I'm some small-town hick or what, but she is just not impressed by me.

I know I'm the new girl, and I'm from out of town, and I'm probably the one on staff with the least experience, but so far, Rebecca just has me running errands, fetching coffee, coordinating meetings, mailing packages—girl Friday kind of stuff.

I mean, I still totally love it. But the closest I've come to actual writing is labeling files. Rebecca makes me write the labels in pencil first, and then go over the pencil with Sharpie. She *may* have some OCD issues. In any case, it's not exactly Pulitzer-track material.

Rebecca keeps me busy, though. Which is good. For a lot of reasons. If nothing else, it means I won't be able to dwell on the one real bummer about spending my summer here in LA—being away from my friends on the Fourth of July.

Ugh, who am I kidding, diary? The bummer is being away from *Archie*.

Polly:

> Hey, sis. You around? I wanna catch up. Also need more details about this 'Rad Brad' of yours. Sounds very . . . Not-Archie. Can't be a bad thing. Miss you.

Betty:

> You too! But you can just call him "Brad." PLEASE.:) Totally not Archie. In a good way. But also not Archie. In a bad way.

"Rad Brad." That's how he introduced himself. It was so deliberately cheesy that I had to laugh, which I'm guessing was the point.

I met him my second week out here. I was finally starting to get used to the energy in LA—the insane traffic, having to sit on the freeway for hours of the day, every day, how the weather is always the same (seriously, no one here knows what to do on the rare chance that it rains. They would FREAK if they had to live through a winter in Riverdale, even if we do have enough maple syrup to keep the whole city on an infinite Master Cleanse) . . . The fact that even the regular people kind of look like celebrities, and maybe they are just celebrities-in-waiting, after all. I still felt like the small-town girl in the big city, because how could I not? Literally *all* my clothes had some kind of flowery pink print on them. It was like wearing a sign on my forehead that said TOURIST . . . or ALIEN. But I was starting to adjust to the city's rhythms, and even though I felt foreign, I also felt comfortable.

Polly kept texting, asking about the guys in LA, and I kept telling her: Guys don't usually notice me. I'm the "sweet" one. The girl next door. And the one guy I've wanted to notice me for ages definitely loves me . . . but probably not in the way that I want. For him, I *am* the girl next door.

(I don't know for sure how he feels. I've always been too afraid to ask.)

So it was a summer Friday, and Rebecca had me picking up sushi for the office (rock shrimp tempura rolls, brown rice, extra-spicy mayo on the side, and a hijiki salad—I knew Rebecca's order by heart, already). But even though I'd called in advance, the host told me it would be a while, so I grabbed my book (*The Bluest Eye,* favorite reread, of course) and settled on the grass at Maguire Gardens, which always has great people-watching.

It was one of those days that even smells like summer: everything green and in bloom, the sky the kind of blue you only ever see in professional photographs. But this was actual, real life. Hashtag no filter.

Suddenly, there was a shadow over the page. "Doing some light reading, huh?"

I looked up. It was a guy who looked about my age, casual in a T-shirt and cargo pants, with sandy blond surfer hair. He was smiling a toothpaste-commercial smile at me.

I flushed. "I guess it's not exactly summer escapist reading, but she's my favorite," I said. Understatement of the century. Toni Morrison is my IDOL. *Hello Giggles* is setting up a signing for her this summer and I'm dying to be a part of it. I've been dropping "subtle" hints—like carrying one of her books on me at all times—since I found out.

"If that's your summer escapist reading, you're going to need another escape," he said. When he smiled, his eyes crinkled up at the corners.

"What do you suggest?" I asked. Was I flirting? Maybe LA Betty could flirt. Maybe Riverdale Betty could learn a thing or two from her.

His eyes crinkled again. "I was hoping you'd ask that. My number-one suggestion is this: You let me take over as your recreational director." I must have looked surprised, because he added, "Or, you know, just a dinner. Low-key. I swear I'm not a psycho killer weirdo. Promise."

"Hmm." I pretended to think about it. "I mean, as long as you're not a psycho killer weirdo. I do like low-key."

"See? We're soul mates."

Soul mates. I had a flash of Archie's mop of red hair, his freckles, and those deep green eyes. But even though Archie and I eat at Pop's together on the regular, those meals could never be mistaken for dates.

"Here's my phone. Can I get your number?" He passed it to me. Then he frowned. "Oh. Also, your name would be nice. I guess I got a little ahead of myself."

I laughed. "It's Betty. Betty Cooper." I took the phone from him, then gasped as I realized the time. Rebecca's rock shrimp tempura would be cold by now. Darn. I punched in my phone number as quickly as I could, grabbed my stuff, and turned to leave. "I'm sorry to rush away, but I have—my internship . . ."

"No problem. You can tell me all about it. At dinner."

I smiled, wondering if my own eyes were crinkling up at the corners, too. "At dinner."

"Oh! And by the way, I'm Brad. Or—since I'm guessing you're new to that SoCal lifestyle—you can call me Rad Brad."

I looked at him. "Okay, but can I also <u>not</u> call you that?" Flirty, LA Betty again! Shocking. And kinda fun.

"Betty Cooper, you can call me anything you want. But you should probably get back to work before your boss catches you picking up surfer dudes on your lunch break."

From: KweenKatJosie@Pussycats.net
To: [list: Bad_Kitties]
Re: Set list for tomorrow

My most exalted goddesses/sisters/singers:

Thank you, both, for crushing it at yesterday's rehearsal. We rule, clearly.

Don't forget, we're meeting at the school today at 2:00 sharp for another sesh before tomorrow night's big show in Town Hall Square. I've attached the set list. Take a look, mark it up, and come prepared to defend any notes or changes you suggest.

Tomorrow we'll meet at the Square at 4:00 for a sound check. Punctuality, ladies. We may not care about making it to the annual Twilight screening of *Independence Day* (does Jughead Jones think he's being ironic or something?), but in typical Pussycat tradition, we need some time to get our preperformance party on.

Last but not least, if either of you see Reggie Mantle around, I suggest you dodge. He's been offering to "manage" the Pussycats. *Don't* let him corner you unless you're looking for a headache today. And we can't afford headaches!

Hugs and hisses,

J

CHAPTER TWO

JUGHEAD

The trailer is always at its most repulsive (or should I say, "squalor chic"?) early in the morning; it's too bad I'm an early riser by nature. The small bit of rising light that struggles to creep in through the dollhouse windows of this place only ends up casting shadows across the sagging, thrift store furniture and lighting up every last corner dust ball. It's practically an artistic homage to neglect.

Already, this morning was no different than any other. Stale cigarette smoke and the smell of cheap beer thickened the air. I peeled myself up to a sitting position on the couch—getting in before Dad last night meant I got to take the couch for myself, literally the absolute least I could do, leaving the bedroom for him—and looked around.

The place was empty. It *felt* empty, too, in that echoey, negative space way that you can't quite articulate, but you understand intrinsically. Some spaces, you can just feel the emptiness in your bones.

Getting in before Dad also meant Dad was out late. And that meant . . .

Well, nothing good.

My parents' constant fighting was awful, and it used to make my stomach cramp to watch them scream and shout in front of Jellybean, in particular, who you could tell was really upset by it. But at least when Mom was yelling at Dad, even if it was awful for Jellybean and me, it meant they were both in the same place, together.

"It's just for a little while," was what she said to me, just before she loaded a beat-up suitcase into the trunk of an even more beat-up used car, strapped Jellybean into the backseat, even though my sister kept insisting she was big enough to ride shotgun, and pulled out. *"Just until your father gets himself together."* As if "together" was something easy, some socially dictated checklist of actions my father would be able to tackle point by point until he somehow, miraculously, became whole again.

As if my father had ever been whole in the first place.

It wasn't that I didn't want to believe in him. Or in them. But at sixteen, I couldn't remember a time when my dad had *ever* been "together." It didn't bode well for my mother's plans.

And the fact that she hadn't asked me to come? I tried not to think about what that meant. Someone had to stay here with Dad, anyway, and keep an eye on his decidedly-not-together existence. So here I was, the opposite-of-prodigal son, left behind, in Riverdale, to keep an eye out.

It would have been easier to keep tabs on Dad if he were ever around. But I guess that's the whole point.

Most kids count down the days until summer vacation. To be honest, though, I missed the structure of the school year, having a rhythm to the days (even if that rhythm sometimes involved pop quizzes and term papers and stuff). Or maybe it was just that *this* summer felt particularly formless, with Mom and Jellybean moving out, and Betty away . . . and Archie all tied up in . . . who even knows, he's *never* around, and it couldn't possibly be because he's working so hard doing construction for his dad. I'm not buying *that*.

Once, Archie and I were practically brothers. Our fathers were partners, and we grew up together. But Archie's different lately. And when I went to find him three weeks ago, to let him know what was going on with my mom—that she had left and taken Jellybean with her? Well, he just wasn't around. Literally. And he didn't respond to any texts. My best friend just . . . ghosted me.

How long is "a little while," anyway?

I showered off some of the scuzz from the humid night and got dressed quickly, stashing my rubbish phone with the cracked screen in one pocket (no messages), and my woefully empty wallet in the other. I was working that night, so it wouldn't be empty for too long, at least. But before I hit the Twilight to get everything ready for our totally-not-ironic July 3 screening of *Independence Day*, I wanted to hear Archie say to my face that we weren't heading to Centerville for the cheesy fireworks and male bonding. (I know, I know— but it's tradition.)

And that meant finding my dad *and* Archie.

Why did I have the feeling that neither of them were going to make that especially easy for me?

∧∧∧

I walked from the trailer to Pop's; not ideal, but I didn't think boosting Dad's truck to find my dad and *ask him if I could borrow his truck* for a road trip would go over so well. (Of course, small-town Riverdale never seems quite as small as it is when you're hoofing it.) When I left, the truck was sitting in front of our house, which meant that Dad had taken his bike (which, side note, was not really all that much better a choice than the truck, if he'd been drinking, but that was a whole other thing that I'd think about later, if ever). Anyway, I left the truck where it was and kept on walking.

I took the long way, which made no sense, unless you knew that I was walking past Archie's block, hoping to get a glimpse of him, and talk about tomorrow night. The street was hushed, rows of houses still dark, waiting quietly for the sun

23

to rise in full. The only window that was lit up was Archie's, actually, which was kind of crazy for how early in the morning it was. I assumed that meant he was awake. But even after waiting a few minutes, feeling like a stalker—*oh, it's just Jughead Jones, skulking away in the shadows like always, just like the freak that he is*—there was no sign of movement up there. I had a clear view of his bed and he wasn't on it.

I sighed and fished my phone out of my pocket. *You up?* I texted, feeling like a creep on a booty call instead of just a regular (if mildly freaky, skulking) guy checking in with a friend. I watched the window intently, but there was nothing. And no message appeared on my screen, not even those torturous little bubbles that tell you, at bare minimum, that there's someone on the other end at least *thinking* about what to say to you. So after a few minutes—more than I'd really care to admit, to be honest—I shrugged, put my phone away, and kept on walking, across town to Pop's.

I had no idea where Archie would be at this hour. I'd say he was with his dad, on-site early for the day's work. That would have been the easy way to rationalize his absence. But it would require pretending I hadn't noticed that Mr. Andrews's truck was still in their driveway. Meaning Mr. Andrews wasn't at work. And if Mr. Andrews wasn't at work, Archie wasn't there, either. Even I couldn't head-canon that cognitive dissonance.

So, where the hell was Archie, anyway?

∿∿∿

By the time I got to Pop's, the sun had risen and I was sticky from the heat. It was still early enough that the parking lot was empty . . . but not completely deserted, like I would have expected. Sartre said, "Hell is other people," and you didn't have to spend much time with me to know that I emphatically agreed.

(I mean, given that motto, you probably wouldn't get to spend much time with me, anyway. And you wouldn't want to if you could.)

Still nothing from Archie. It wouldn't have been weird, given how early it was, except that I *knew* he wasn't at home, which meant he had to be awake. Just more fodder for the enigma that Archie Andrews had become.

The last time I even saw him in person was at Pop's, actually. A week ago to the day. It was, as they say, a dark and stormy night, and I was huddled in a booth, alone, trying to write. I've been doing more and more of that lately. I have no idea if my writing is any good—probably not, who are we kidding?—but I kind of don't care. When I'm writing, I can tune the world out, and at the same time, process things. It's the best of all possible worlds, for me.

Of course, I realize that "it was a dark and stormy night" is maybe the *most* cliché way for a writer to set the stage for his story, but, you know—write your truth and all that. So it was dark and stormy out that night. I can't help the way it was outside.

Pop teased me for spending so much time alone, in a booth, hunched over my clunky old laptop—you'd think he'd be used to it by now—but he was giving me extra grief that night, telling me if I spent any more time holed up with my writing (even if I was technically out in public), I'd turn into a character from a horror movie, like the guy from *The Shining* or worse.

I told him, "Guys like that don't live in Riverdale." I believed it then. Though, soon enough, I'd learn differently.

It was such a mess outside that, for hours, it was just Pop and me in the diner. A few people stopped in for takeout orders, but it was pretty clear Pop was keeping the place open just so I'd have somewhere to be. He's a good guy, and I didn't want to wear out my welcome. I was starting to think about packing up and heading out—wondering if I was going to go back to the trailer, where Mom and Jellybean's absence lingered like a stain that bleach couldn't completely kill, or where else I could possibly go—when the overhead bell chimed and someone walked in.

I heard Pop say it—"Archie! Look what the cat dragged in! What are you doing out in this mess?"—before I could look up and see who it was.

"Jughead." Archie's hair was clumped to his forehead with rain, and a little puddle was forming at his feet. He didn't look like something the cat dragged in; he looked like something that had been dragged through *hell,* and the rain was only part of it. There was a distracted look in his eyes. No, worse than *distracted.* Maybe even *haunted.*

"Hey," I said, not sure how to react to him. After a second, watching raindrops gather at his fingertips and slide toward the floor, I gestured. "You wanna sit?"

He looked hesitant, which was definitely a twist of the knife. There was a time when I wouldn't have had to ask, and he wouldn't have thought twice. And it wasn't so long ago.

One summer can change everything, I guess.

I shrugged like I didn't care and tried to make myself believe it. He sat down. "Hey."

"Long time no see," I said, since apparently I was *only* thinking in clichés that night. "What've you been up to?"

"Working for my dad, you know. Pouring concrete." He grimaced. "It's not exactly my dream job, but Dad needs the help. Anyway."

"Anyway," I agreed. *My* dad worked for Mr. Andrews; Archie didn't have to tell me how grueling the job was.

"And . . . you're still writing," he went on, nodding at the laptop in front of me.

"Trying. It's not exactly National Book Award material. Who knows if anyone will ever want to read this stuff."

His face went softer, like he was thinking of something far away. "Come on. Of course they will. You were always the best at making up stories. Remember all those campouts we had in the tree house? Your ghost stories were always the scariest. I had to pretend I wasn't terrified. Half the time I wanted to run back into the house and hide under my bed with Vegas."

I smiled. "Yeah, I remember. And you sucked at pretending . . ."

I could read you like a book then, Arch, I thought. *Still can.* Construction didn't explain why we'd drifted, why he was never around. And it didn't explain the sad, distracted look on his face.

"Hey," he said suddenly, looking a little eager, but also shy. "What if I told you . . . I'd been doing some writing, too?" He glanced down at the table, like this was the most embarrassing thing he could possibly have revealed to me.

"No way." He didn't have to be embarrassed, but it was still a surprise. Football jock Archie writing? *Unexpected* was an understatement. "Like a novel or something?"

"Uh, more like poetry," he said, turning a little bit red.

"Poetry? You?"

"Yeah, I don't know. More like, maybe . . . song lyrics?" Now he looked completely mortified. He waved his hand. "Forget it. Anyway." His little moment of vulnerability was over. "What are you doing for the Fourth?"

"*Independence Day* at the Twilight on the third, as tradition dictates. But we're closed on the Fourth, so I have the day off."

"Right, of course. Nice." He ran a hand through his hair, thoughtful.

I have no idea what possessed me to say what I did. I'd been thinking about it for weeks—hell, it was on my mind when I woke up this morning. But things with Archie felt too broken. I was going to let it go. And then I changed my mind.

Maybe it was that wistful look on his face. Maybe it was the talk about the tree house, about how far back he and I go. "Remember when we used to go down to Centerville every year to watch the fireworks?"

"Good times."

"Why don't we do it again this year? Take the bus down? A blast from the past."

I had a little flash of nerves, like it'd be a punch in the stomach if he said no. But his eyes brightened. "Yeah. Yeah, that sounds like a plan! Come by my house at four?"

"You got it," I said, and for a second it felt like everything between us was exactly the same as it'd always been.

It was sickening, how much I wanted that to be true. By the time I realized where Archie and I really stood, exactly how precarious our old, familiar friendship had become . . . well, by then it was too late to be anything but over it.

SWEETWATER RIVER FISHING REPORT
FOR JULY 4

Water flow: 711 CFS

Visibility: 36 inches

Water temperature at midday: 51°F

Water condition: Clear

Best time of day to fish: Late mornings to early evenings

Best stretch: Stretch beyond Striker's Cove

Best access point: Park at base of campground entrance,

3.4 mi. hike down.

Fish species: Trout

Fishing season: April 1 through November 30

Recommended fly fishing tippet: 4X Tippet

Best fly fishing rod: 9' 5 Weight Fly Rod

Best floating fly line: WF Trout Fly Line

Best sinking fly line: Class V Sink Tip Fly Line

* * *

From the office of the Riverdale Mayor and the

Town Parks & Recreation Department,

have a great holiday and BE SAFE!

CHAPTER THREE

VERONICA

"The early bird gets the worm, *m'hija*," Daddykins always says. But honestly—what's so appealing about that? Um, *worms*? I'd just as soon sleep in.

So you can imagine how irate I was to find Mother looming over me like some kind of incredibly beautiful, perfectly coiffed ogre, having snapped up the window shade of my cabin, shaking my shoulders gently and tapping a sensible Valentino flat against the floor. "Ronnie, we're leaving," she said, an impatient edge creeping into her tone. "Soon. You know your father's on a schedule. Katie, I'm sorry, but you'll have to go."

I glanced at my Cartier watch—a little trinket from Daddy, of course. It was barely 7 a.m. Simply uncivilized.

"Unless, Katie"—ugh, my mouth felt dry and cottony, my head pounding from last night's fun—"unless you want to come with? Last chance to change your mind. Are you *really* going to skip the party of the summer?"

Gingerly, squinting against the sunlight, I rolled to one side and propped myself up on an elbow. I arched an eyebrow at my best friend, who'd slept, like so many summer nights before, in the extra bed in my cabin after the previous night's festivities had gone on longer than anticipated. Katie stayed over so often she kept her own tub of La Mer in every Lodge bathroom.

Katie smiled at me, flashing blindingly white teeth courtesy of the finest orthodontia the Upper East Side had to offer.

"But, Veronica," she purred, teasing, "I *am* going to be at the party of the summer. Kelly Klein's annual East Hampton Fourth of July party is legendary. Last year she had an American flag donut wall. And supposedly Rihanna's going to be there."

I snorted. "Rihanna? Please. If you're lucky, *maybe* you'll spot a wayward Kardashian. You can't throw a Louboutin on the East End without hitting one. And if I'd known you were all about the themed eats, I could have custom ordered you red, white, and blue macarons from Ladurée. You know Claude gave his personal cell to our chef."

"Don't be silly, Veronica—*you* know our menu has been set for months." That was Mother's interjection, a smile in her brown eyes giving her away. Her mouth was still a firm line, though.

"Katie, dear, you know we'd love to have you. But if you're staying in the Hamptons, it's time to start saying your good-byes. The Captain wants to leave in thirty minutes. At Mr. Lodge's request."

We all know that Mr. Lodge's "requests" are anything but.

I groaned. "Mother, that's barely enough time for a double-shot cappuccino—which we both desperately need."

Katie nodded at this and batted puppy-dog eyes. "That and an industrial-sized dose of aspirin," she said, rubbing her temples.

Mother ignored Katie's dramatics, folding her arms across her chest. "I'll send Marta down with coffee and Advil. And I can probably get your father to forty-five minutes. But no promises, so"—she gave a little waving "hurry up" gesture—"get to it."

"Ask him for an hour. Then he'll give you—*us*—our forty-five." I grinned.

Say what you will about Daddy—and there's plenty to say—but he does love a good negotiation. Even more than negotiating? Daddy loves a loophole. So much so that he actually named his yacht the *SS Loophole*. And like any other loophole, this boat was great at getting us exactly where we wanted to be.

Katie and I got dressed quickly, Katie shimmying out of a borrowed pair of pajamas and back into the Stella McCartney sundress she'd been wearing to last night's hang.

"I smell like a bonfire," she said, shaking her tanned arms through the ruffled off-the-shoulder sleeves.

"Girl, if you smell like last night, you know it was a good night," I said. At least she came by it honestly; Luke's impromptu Georgica Pond clambake was *epic*. Like, blow your curfew, forget all about whoever your summer crush has been until tonight, and slap another coat of lip gloss on epic.

We both laughed. Katie's been my partner in crime since the first day of kindergarten at Spence. Her mom's a little bit psycho—nice, but psycho—and even back then wouldn't let Katie go anywhere near a molecule of gluten. Whereas *my* mother sent me to school with a Magnolia cupcake in a plastic container, along with a gourmet PB&J from Blue Ribbon Bakery, may it rest in peace. Poor Katie looked so mournful at the sight of those delicacies that I gave her half of everything in my lunch bag . . . And sharing does *not* come easily to me, so you know it was kismet.

We've been inseparable ever since. Save for my family's annual Fourth of July cocktails at our penthouse in the Dakota. Katie's been crushing on Luke Chastain's best friend, the improbably named Mac—an Australian transplant with killer abs and a delicious accent—for the last three years. And Luke and Mac spend the Fourth in the Hamptons, silly boys, which means Katie does, too.

It's okay. It just means more for *moi*. And there's always texting and FaceTime to keep up-to-date on anything urgent.

So while most people were crammed onto jitneys, trains, or the interminable parking lot that is the LIE, the *SS Loophole* was speeding away from Sag Harbor port back to New York City.

I didn't blame Katie for wanting to stay out east—Mac *did* have those abs, after all—but you couldn't have paid me to join her. Kardashians and donut walls are all well and good, but everyone knows no one does a bash like the Lodges do. Our annual Fourth of July party was no exception. We'd been hosting it for as long as I can remember. Even as a preschooler, I understood the extra level of prestige that went along with the effort of coming home from your tony beach house just for the night, having scored an invite to one of the most exclusive events of the season. Being on the Lodges' list was a status symbol on par with an invite to Warhol's Factory, once upon a time. Tomorrow night I'd be clinking glasses with Du Ponts, Rockefellers, Vanderbilts . . . and *we'd* be the most important name in the room.

I know what you're thinking: I'm a spoiled girl living a charmed life.

You're 100 percent correct. And I make no apologies.

Daddy works insanely hard to provide us with this lifestyle, and if he wants to lavish the spoils of his work on his doting daughter and devoted wife, why not?

And if my life is good, then summer in New York is the ne plus ultra. It's dreadfully hot, so steamy you can practically see the lines of heat shimmering off the sidewalk in waves. That's where East Hampton escapes come in. Daddy designed our eight-bedroom, shingle-style mansion—"Lodgehampton," as locals know it—from the ground up, with no detail forgotten. I have my own suite in the south wing overlooking the back garden and heated saltwater pool. Beyond that, it's a short wooden path to our private beach access. The house has central AC, but I usually sleep with the windows open just to hear the ocean waves crash. Who needs a white noise machine when you have the real thing?

Most summers, Katie and I would throw a few sundresses into a bag the second that school let out and decamp for Lodgehampton until Labor Day. It was easy enough to get back to the city with the boat, or if Daddy was using that, a helicopter charter. But this summer, I'd been going back and forth much more—and loving every second of it. It was the best of both worlds.

Daddy doesn't work as much in the summer, which is divine. We get to have leisurely family meals together and Le Cirque on Fridays. At home, in our prewar classic six, Marta always has a table or a high ball cart prepared just so. And this summer, I'd at long last joined the masses of typical American teens in a manner wholly unexpected:

This summer, I had a job.

Mind you, I was working at *Vogue*. So maybe not completely typical teen stuff. Technically, I was a fashion intern, but after my first week on staff, I'd been scooped up to work as personal assistant to Grace Coddington.

(I know!)

I guess that woman really does recognize style when she sees it.

The job was tailor-made for me; Grace and I were so alike, I could anticipate her needs before she did. (She starts her day with a matcha green tea latte, no sugar, at 9:30 a.m. on the dot, and she always drinks a decaf of the same at 3, preferably with a Millefoglie from Sant Ambroeus. She *always* takes calls from Anna, never from press. And woe to the assistant who shows her page layouts without proofing typos first.) I had access to the magazine's infamous closet— Mecca, practically—and managed to squeeze in a little shopping of my own in between errands (Nelle at Barneys has all of my sizes and cosmetics colors on file).

All that, and they're incredibly flexible about scheduling. Meaning I'm free to spend extra-long weekends at Lodgehampton, and take off afternoons to help Mother prepare for our party.

You can see why my work feels so much like play.

"*M'hija*, you're grinning like the cat that ate the canary."

"Hmm?" We were stretched out on the rear deck of the

boat, cupping foamy cappuccinos to protect them from the wind as the boat cut smoothly through the water. I sat up and crossed my legs so I was facing her.

"Just thinking about how lucky we are, I guess. Looking forward to the holiday. The party. It would be hard not to smile, surrounded by all this . . ." I gestured at the expanse of clean, squishy white cushions, the brilliant sunlight, the green-blue water surrounding us on all sides. "I may be a little bit pampered"—Mom gave an uncharacteristically indelicate snort at this—"but I'm not a sociopath."

"Glad to hear it," she said, sincere. "We *are* lucky to have all of this, of course. And we should be grateful. But we have nothing if we don't have . . ." She eyed me, prompting me to finish the thought.

"Family," I said on cue.

"Family," she echoed. She finished her coffee and licked a fluff of foam from her lip. "Now, for the party decor—"

"Well, I already know you're not impressed by Kelly Klein's donut wall," I said, laughing. "But the macarons?"

"Well, if they're from Ladurée, they could never be tacky, but we can be more inspired. *Quality always.*" Our motto, and I mouthed the words along with her. "In any case, as I told you, it's all mostly set. Rafe sent over the book with all of the party details last week. Sparklers instead of swizzle sticks for the cocktails. Nautical wreaths with red, white, and blue threading. Mini lobster rolls and ahi tacos in wax paper served on the balconies."

"Urban picnic, I love it," I gushed. "I'll get the book and we can go over today's game plan." I loved that our designer didn't use Pinterest or Instagram; analog was his appeal. It made his creations that much more unexpected . . . and exclusive.

I slid off the cushions and padded down the deck through the saloon and down the stairs to my parents' cabin. I stopped just outside the door, though. Daddy was on the phone, and he didn't sound happy.

"And when were you going to tell me about this?" he was saying, his voice low but shaking with anger. He paused, listening to something from the other side of the conversation. "That's not good enough. Those payments—"

The boat rocked suddenly, as we passed through choppy waters. I lost my balance at the same time as Daddy's door swung open. The expression in his eyes went blank as he took me in. "I'll have to call you back," he said tersely, and hung up without waiting for a response.

"M'hija," he said, turning to me as he slid his phone into his pocket. "Can I help you with something?"

"I, uh, was just looking for Rafe's book for the party. Mom and I were going to go over last-minute details, figure out the day. I'm sorry, I didn't mean to disturb you," I stammered. Forceful phone calls were hardly new for Daddy, but there'd been something in his voice just now—a desperate pitch to his anger that wasn't normal.

Or was I just imagining things?

"Have a look," he said, and stepped out of my way so I could move to Mother's nightstand. As I passed by, he ran a palm over the back of my head, like I was a little girl he was tucking in at night.

I froze. "Is . . . is something wrong, Daddy?"

"Of course not," he said without hesitation. "There's nothing to worry about. You grab the book and get back to your mother. It's going to be our most magical Fourth of July ever."

"Okay," I said. I tried to sound like I meant it. *You're just imagining things*, I insisted in my head.

But somehow, it didn't quite feel true.

CHAPTER FOUR

ARCHIE

I never thought of myself as a complicated guy. What you see is what you get: Small-town high school kid. Football, family dinners, milk shakes with my friends at Pop's after school. You get the picture.

Summers were always the same: long days swimming in Sweetwater River with Betty, movies at the Twilight with Jughead at night. Extra-long Frisbee tosses with Vegas. Dad grilling burgers at dusk—usually dropping one, which was great for Vegas, but a pain for Mom and me, who were usually starving by then.

But things change, I guess, even in a small town like Riverdale where you think nothing ever does. And I should know. Because Mom left two years ago, and she hasn't come back.

That was hard enough. And this summer, things are weird. Betty's off in LA, which is so great for her. But I have to admit, I miss her like crazy. And Jug and I . . . well, we're not really hanging out that much. It's mostly my fault, I guess. Because . . . well, because of other stuff happening that I never expected. The kind of stuff that changes everything.

When I was little, I liked to play "what if?" *"What if I'm still awake when Mom comes upstairs?"* (She read me an extra bedtime story.) *"What if I enter Vegas in that dog show?"* (That was Betty's suggestion. But he threw up on the judges, so no prizes for us.) *"What if I try out for little league even if I'm nervous?"* (Little Archie made shortstop!)

But as you get older, the stakes of the "what if?" game get higher. What if I'd gone with Mom when she left, instead of staying with Dad? For once, I'd know what it was like to be in a big city, what life outside of Riverdale really had to offer.

But on the flip side, what if Dad didn't have me around this summer to help with his business? He pretended he was just making work for me, doing me a favor, letting me pour concrete and stuff. But I know better. I've seen him at night, hunched over the dining room table with a calculator and a stack of bills in his hands. I hear him on the phone, trying to haggle with vendors or chase payments from clients. It's a tough time for construction. Having me around means one extra pair of hands, one less salary to scrounge up.

Then there are the smaller things, the ones that have ripple effects you can't possibly see coming. What if Dad hadn't decided to clean out the garage that first week of the summer? Where would I be, then?

I thought he was crazy. It was insanely hot, the kind of weather that breaks records and turns into the only thing anyone wants to talk about. But Dad didn't care; when he set his mind to something, that was that. So there we were, on a hazy June evening, my arms, neck, back burning from a ten-hour shift, holed up in the stuffy garage. It was hot as an oven and smelled like dust and gasoline.

"Do we have to do this now?" I groaned. I was collapsed into an ancient lawn chair. I could barely keep my eyes open. "I'm dead. Aren't you dead? How are you not dead?" This was earlier in the summer, before I'd started to fill out, so I couldn't keep up with the work without coming home ten kinds of sore.

Dad laughed at me. "Son, when you're my age, *dead* is kind of the default. You learn to push through. Try it."

"All right, all right." I eased myself out of the chair reluctantly. "Don't say I never did anything for you."

"You know what they say, Arch," he said, pulling a sagging cardboard box from the corner. "One man's trash is another man's—"

"Soviet-era melon baller?" I shook my head at what he was holding up. I'd only ever seen them on TV shows set in the '60s. "Come on, Dad. Are you serious?"

Dad frowned. "Hmm. Better throw that in the 'keep' pile."

"What?" He was hopeless, so I had to jump in. "Don't be crazy. I'll start a pile for the Salvation Army." I grabbed the melon baller out of his hands before he could argue, even though my shoulders twinged with every move.

One scooter with a broken wheel, one terrifying stuffed clown that was definitely haunted, and three stacks of musty comic books (those I kept) later, and there it was, staring at me from the bottom of a box: a photo of the whole family. Mom, Dad, and me. Even Vegas was there, his tongue hanging out of his mouth like it does when he gets excited. In the photo we were all smiling. Dad had an arm around Mom and she was hugging me.

Was that when it started? Whatever it was that told her she'd be better off without us? Was this photo a clue? Dad looking at her, but her looking straight ahead? Should we have known? Seen it coming?

"Uh, hey, Dad," I started, uneasy, "I've been meaning to ask . . . Have you talked to Mom recently?" Maybe they'd been in secret contact all along. Maybe she knew he was struggling with the business. Maybe she'd been planning to come back, and she was packing a bag right then.

The "what if?" game again.

Dad stiffened. "She's pretty busy. You know, she just started that job with that new firm."

"Right." I'd been trying not to think about that. New job meant she was planning to stay a while. Even I couldn't pretend differently. "So, I take that as a no."

"Hey!" For a second, I thought Dad was responding to me, like he was upset that I'd even brought it up or something. But when I looked over, his eyes were shiny and he was pulling something big and bulky out of a box. "Now, *here's* something worth hanging on to. My old Stratocaster."

"Whoa." Even I knew a vintage piece when I saw it. It was green, glossy, even-coated with garage grime, with a white fretboard that was scratched and worn through the mother-of-pearl inlay. Some of the strings were loose, and a few were missing. But even with all of that .... it was a thing of major beauty. "Dad, you used to play?"

My dad was a musician, once upon a time? *How* had that never come up? It was like I had to rethink everything I thought I knew about the old man.

What if he'd been *cool*, once?

"Oh, now and again," he said, strumming the saggy strings. They made a quiet little pinging sound that made me desperate to plug the thing in and let 'er rip.

"That's *sick* Dad. The good sick, I mean. Can I try it?" Suddenly, there was nothing I wanted more.

Dad gave me a look. "You should know never to touch another man's guitar, Arch! Besides, I bought you your own. Remember?"

I remembered. He gave it to me for my sixteenth birthday. An acoustic Gibson in a dark wood that was solid and heavy when you held it. I played well enough . . . but never outside my own bedroom. The idea of playing for other people made me break into a cold sweat.

You could call it stage fright, but a part of me wondered . . . was I just waiting for my inspiration? And *what if* . . . it never came along?

But it turned out, I didn't have to worry about that.

∿∿∿

"Earth to Archie? What's going on in there?"

"Huh?" I blinked. The sun was coming up, lighting up Ms. Grundy—Geraldine's—picture window. She stood in front of it like a shadow, with a confused look on her face. The sun made her hair glow. *Your hair glowing in the sunlight.* Hmm. Maybe that was a song lyric? I couldn't stop thinking in lyrics around her. She just had that effect on me. God, *I* was a character from a cheesy love song. "Oh, sorry, I guess I was just thinking."

"Must've been some deep thoughts." She smiled. "You were in a trance, there."

I was. Playing that "what if?" game again. *What if* Betty hadn't gone to LA, and my Dad hadn't asked me to come work for him? What if we'd never dug up that old guitar so

I'd take up playing again, even if I was only playing for myself? What if I hadn't been walking home from work alone that hot, humid day late in June, when a light blue VW Bug that I didn't recognize pulled up . . . ?

"Archie Andrews? What are you doing, walking in this heat?"

I squinted. The woman behind the wheel had wavy, dark blond hair and worried-looking eyes behind sunglasses. Ms. Grundy! Riverdale High's music teacher. I almost didn't recognize her outside of school and not all buttoned-up the way she was when she was working. "Umm, building character?" It sounded silly when I said it, and we both laughed.

"Well, hop in before you die of heatstroke," she said, leaning across the seat to open the door for me.

That day, she dropped me straight at home. I didn't think much of it, except for how weird it always was to see teachers out in real life. But the next day, she was waiting for me just past the construction site again, like she'd actually planned to drive me home. And then the next day, she was there again, and after that, it was like we'd just come to some unspoken agreement.

There's a part of me that will always think it was fate, running into her that day. Because suddenly I had a person to talk to about the guitar . . . and the songs I'd started writing—just scribbles, mostly, at first. She saw the guitar on my porch one afternoon and asked me if I played.

I was worried that I wouldn't be good enough for her. I tried to protest, but she insisted. I was scared she'd run away, and I'd be right back where I started, alone.

But she listened and took me seriously. She saw something in me that no one else had, not even Betty. When I played for her, she smiled at me and . . . everything made sense.

"You have potential, Archie," she told me. "Have you considered private lessons?"

We both knew what she was really asking. And we both knew the answer to that: yes.

Eventually, we were sharing . . . other things. One afternoon, without saying a word, Geraldine took an unexpected turn on our way home. The next thing I knew, she'd parked the car down a little hideaway bank of the Sweetwater River. Soon it became our place.

Maybe—probably—a part of me knew what we were doing was wrong (she was a teacher, after all—it was probably even illegal, even though it was what we both wanted), but it didn't matter. As time went on, my feelings for her became stronger than for anyone I'd ever met before. Soon she was the most important person in my life.

That was why I'd come running over this morning (literally, I was still in my sweaty Riverdale gym shorts, which maybe wasn't so romantic, but it was the easiest way to get to her first thing in the morning without raising any suspicions). It was July 3, the holiday was here, and I wanted to do something special with her. I wanted to be with her, always.

I turned to Geraldine now. "I was just thinking about the Fourth," I started, feeling a little nervous, even though I didn't know why. "Uh . . . are you doing anything for the holiday?"

Geraldine gave a little smirk while she poured herself a cup of coffee. "Actually, I was going to go camping down by the river . . ." She took a sip. "Want to come?"

We both knew the answer to that, too.

Archie:

Found tent. Buried in the garage. All set!

Geraldine:

Can't wait. Meet here after dinner, we'll head to the woods?

Archie:

y

Geraldine:

[DELETE THREAD?] [Y]

CHAPTER FIVE

BETTY

Dear Diary:

You will never believe what just happened. I can't believe it. That's not an exaggeration; I am literally hiding in the *Hello Giggles* supply closet writing this all down because when I pinched myself, it still didn't make it more real.

I'm finally, *finally* getting my first big break here.

When I woke up this morning, all I was thinking about was how strange it was to be spending the Fourth of July away from my friends, away from my family . . . away from Riverdale. Good strange, but still. I have plans to meet Brad tonight, but otherwise, my time here is always pretty wide open. Just one big adventure, like I'd hoped.

Hiking in the morning, showering in Aunt Gertrude's guest bathroom with the funny lace skirt around the tissue box, digging up a pair of skinny jeans and a tank that's as "LA" as my wardrobe gets . . . sitting in thirty minutes of traffic just to go three miles on the 405 . . . all pretty standard stuff.

But when I got to the office, there was a totally different vibe than usual. For starters, it was quiet. The clean, bright white of the reception desk was still, and there weren't any phones ringing.

"Hello?" I called out, tiptoeing in carefully like I was afraid of surprising anyone.

The lounge area, usually chill central, was empty. Normally, you'd find at least two writers draped over the peacock-blue midcentury chairs, or browsing the bright yellow bookshelves. Instead, I saw a lone iPad resting on a table, its owner nowhere to be found.

I tentatively made my way into the bullpen. "Oh, hi." It was Cleo, the features editor, hunched over her desk and gnawing on a pink glitter pencil. "It's . . . where is everyone?"

Cleo tapped her pencil on her desk and looked up at me. Her eyes were giant behind the big red frames of her glasses. "Holiday," she shrugged. "People go away. I'm actually leaving for Palm Springs in"—she consulted the Apple Watch on her wrist—"an hour."

"Oh." I scanned the rest of the office. No signs of life. "Is anyone else here at all?" I kind of relished the idea of being alone here, to be honest. There was always plenty of filing or random emails to sort, and the idea of doing it without Rebecca hunched over my back sounded pretty . . . peaceful.

Cleo made a "duh" face. "Rebecca's in the conference room going over wallpaper and fabric swatches for the living room makeover challenge."

"Right, of course." That little bloom of hope deflated. Of course Rebecca wasn't the type to miss work because of a holiday.

I headed into the conference room to deliver her lunch. The door was ajar, and I knocked lightly so it wouldn't seem like I was just barging in.

"Come in."

I did, walking softly. For some reason, just being in Rebecca's presence sent me into tiptoe mode. "I have the lunch order." The paper bag made a deafening rustle as I put it down.

Rebecca was by the back wall, swiveling her gaze back and forth from several different wallpaper swatches: blue flowery, purple flowery, green flowery, and metallic flowery. Flowers of all sizes and shapes, from pop art to Laura Ashley Queen Anne's lace. There was obviously some kind of theme happening.

She sighed. "I don't know. Do you think it's . . . too much?"

Rebecca had never actually asked my opinion about anything before, not so baldly, anyway. "What? Me?" I coughed. "I mean, the wallpaper?"

She turned and rolled her eyes, but nicely enough. "Yes. I mean, florals . . . overdone?"

"I never think so," I answered honestly.

She flicked her eyes over my clothing. "Well, sure. But . . . ugh, the metallic. On the one hand, it's the most interesting of them all. But on the other hand . . ."

She seemed to be waiting for me to say something. "It's a little . . . loud?" We try not to put out any negative energy at *Hello Giggles*, so constructive criticism always has to be very thoughtfully parsed.

"Yes! Loud!" She seemed deeply relieved that I'd found the right wording. "Also, I just read on *Design Sponge* that woodwork is the new wallpaper and"—another heavy sigh—"I don't know, I'm just not feeling this at all. It seems so *uninspired*."

She really did look utterly bored and bereft. She probably never would have even been this open with me in the first place, if it weren't for the holiday and the fact that I was basically the only one around. But who cared? Rebecca was finally talking to me! Asking *my* opinion!

She slumped down at the conference table and rifled through the bag of food, digging out her order. I stood awkwardly for a second, not sure what to do next.

"What did you get?" Rebecca asked. "Something, right? You have to eat. Or, I don't know, maybe you're an aspiring actress and you don't eat. Stranger things happen in this town."

"No, I definitely eat," I assured her. Tentatively, I took out my own food. There aren't many (read: any) sushi restaurants in Riverdale, and I learned very quickly that a spicy tuna roll and side of edamame are two of my favorite things about LA.

Rebecca hadn't come out and asked me to sit with her, sure, but close enough. And I might never get another chance like this again. I decided to go for it, pulling out a chair for myself. LA Betty—flirtier and more daring than my usual, girl-next-door self—was having lunch with her boss.

Rebecca kept up a steady stream of sighing and drumming her fingers on the conference table in between bites. The space between us began to feel squishy and thick, like a thundercloud. It wasn't a comfortable silence. Daring, LA Betty decided—why not, given the day she was having?—to jump in.

"So, woodwork is the new wallpaper, huh?" Brilliant, scintillating commentary, Cooper. I winced, wanting to hide under the table until it was time to go home. But this was LA Betty, who doesn't hide. I pushed on.

"Is that like . . . beadboard? And . . . shiplap?" I wracked my brain thinking back to those home improvement shows Polly likes to watch on lazy Sundays. "But I heard that ship-lap is overdone?" At least, that's what the redhead with the perfect ringlets on *Home Helpers* said once. I think. Honestly, I wasn't sure what shiplap was.

Rebecca perked right up. "It *is* overdone! Girl, we are on the same wavelength."

Thank you, *Home Helpers*. And Polly's mindless binge-TV habits.

"But research shows that our readers love things like temporary wallpaper because it's such an easy way to transform their space without annoying parents, RAs, or landlords. SO"—she waved an arm out—"ALL the florals."

"Right, but . . ." More HGTV trivia seeped from some far-flung corner of my brain. "They have sticky paper that looks like woodwork. And exposed brick. Even concrete, if you're into that industrial vibe." I smiled. "There is shiplap-patterned wallpaper in this world."

Rebecca shrieked. "Genius. Love. Great, this story's yours."

I nearly choked on an edamame bean. "What? I mean, great! Thanks! That's awesome! I won't let you down." I was gushing, this was as embarrassing as being too shy, too tenta-tive. Where was my "happy medium" button?

But Rebecca just laughed. "It's two hundred words about wallpaper. I'm not worried."

"Cool." I took a deep breath. Chill, LA Betty. You're in.

"But, actually, as long as you're here, there is something else you could help out with. I'm really in a bind. As you can see, it's dead here today. And I can't get the 'remote workers' on the line. Obvi they're all very busy getting a head start at 'remote working' on their holiday tans."

I've never been more grateful for my pathological sun-protection habits.

"Of course, anything."

"It's for our lifestyle section. It just landed in our lap from fashion. Supposedly, the fashion editor got a lead that Grace Coddington has a hot young protégé intern at *Vogue* for the summer. Normally, I'd say, who cares? Socialites are a dime a dozen. But this girl's the real deal, the next Olivia Palermo in terms of influence. Nobody below the age of twenty-one in New York City sneezes—or buys a new lip stain—without her approval."

Um, terrifying. "So, a profile?"

"An interview, yeah. But it's gotta be stat, for real—I want it up tonight, midnight latest. Her family does this Fourth of July thing that's the ultimate scene. I mean, people come in from Montauk for this thing. You could go from New York to LA in less time!" She was practically speaking a foreign language, but I nodded my head knowingly.

"So I want a focus on that. Last year, BuzzFeed scooped us with photos of Kelly Klein's American flag donut wall. This will be bigger." Her eyes narrowed. "It *needs* to be."

I had no idea the niche area of socialite lifestyle reporting was so cutthroat. (It made me glad I wasn't here for that whole donut-wall debacle, whatever *that* was.) But I was on it. This wasn't the big break into journalism I'd been hoping for, but an open door is an open door. And LA Betty, apparently, is all about jumping in with both feet.

(And mixing metaphors. Which I'd have to work on before I PUBLISHED MY FIRST PIECE ON *HELLO GIGGLES!*)

"Bigger. Of course. And I'll file it by midnight, no problem." An image of Rad Brad flashed in my brain, but I'd find a way to juggle both, whatever. I didn't want to pass either up. "So who's this new It Girl I need to track down?"

"Here." Rebecca scribbled something on a Post-it and passed it to me. "That's her private cell. If anyone asks, we got it from . . . Well, if anyone asks how we got the number, just play dumb."

"Right." I looked down at the Post-it. Bold letters screamed back at me: This is your big break, LA Betty. Get it done.

Even the name sounded imperious, official. Nobody in New York sneezes without her approval. And *I* had to get her to talk:

VERONICA LODGE.

Kevin:

You gonna be at the Twilight tonight?

Moose:

Yeah, Midge never misses the Independence Day thing.

Kevin:

. . .

Moose:

But . . .

Moose:

. . .

Kevin:

?

Moose:

Maybe we could meet up after?

Kevin:

We'll see.

CHAPTER SIX

JUGHEAD

If Riverdale never changes, then Pop's Chock'Lit Shoppe is its most immutable icon. That glowing neon sign is practically a landmark unto itself. They should enter it in the historical register. I don't even want to think how many hours I've spent with my butt glued to a vinyl diner booth. Or how many burgers Pop's put on my running "tab."

I'm gonna pay it, of course. As soon as I can. I just need to figure out how. Easier said than done. Archie works for his dad. *My* dad . . . well, in theory, my dad works for Archie's dad, too. That's the story, anyway. We're on such different schedules these days, I never see him around. My Spidey-sense tells me that's not a great thing.

Archie, my dad . . . is *everyone* fading away from me this summer?

Maybe I'm wrong about things never changing in Riverdale. It's like that poem, "Nothing Gold Can Stay."

Is it any wonder Pop's has become my home away from home? It's always open, and Pop is always behind the counter. One constant, at least.

Like I said, the lot was empty-ish but not abandoned that morning; as I got closer, I saw Jason Blossom leaning against the side of the building, hunched over a phone, texting furiously. His skin seemed extra pale, translucent, even, in the dawning sun. He was frowning.

"Hey," I said as I drew closer. He glanced up, gave me a quick once-over. His expression was totally inscrutable.

Jason and I run in very different crowds. He's the kind of guy who's . . . never been especially happy to see me, and this morning was no exception. I didn't take it personally. Honestly, standing there in the blinding sunlight, he reminded me of a ghost.

"Texting your adoring fans?" It was a weird thing to say. But then again, Jason was on varsity water polo—at least two-thirds of the female student body crushed on him at some point in their tenure at Riverdale High.

"Uh, sure." He went back to his phone, tapping away. I couldn't get a read on his energy—hyper, alert, eager, but also distracted, preoccupied, nervous. It was too many feelings for one body, if you ask me. I'm not sure he even realized I was still standing there. I took the hint.

The bell over the front door jangled as I walked into the diner. Pop was wiping down the counter, but he looked up and gave me a broad smile that made up for Jason's total lack of interest. "Jughead Jones! I had a feeling you'd be stopping in."

"Am I that predictable, Pop?"

"Predictability is good for business, boy."

"I think that's only true for customers who pay their tabs," I replied, sheepish.

He waved me away. "I'm not worried. We'll square up soon enough." He filled a mug with coffee, black, and slid it toward me. "Now, is it too early in the day for a hamburger?"

I rolled my eyes. "Never."

∧∧∧

Double cheeseburger, medium rare, pink on the inside with the cheddar oozing sticky on the (untoasted, *never* toasted) bun. Pickles, tomatoes, maybe an onion, but no lettuce—it's just water in crunchy form. That was my order, and of course, Pop knew it by heart. Never mind that the sun had barely risen, I ate like I didn't know where my next meal might come from (even though we all knew it would probably be this exact same meal, at this exact same place). My clunky, trusty old laptop sat on the counter next to me, but I hadn't opened it yet. I was mostly concentrating on the food.

"Are those fries crispy enough for you?" Pop asked, refilling my water. I liked them so overcooked they were basically burnt. I held a perfect specimen up to him in a "cheers" gesture and wolfed it down.

"A-plus as usual." I shoveled another handful in.

"Careful. You don't slow down and actually chew, you're going to choke. And I don't want to be responsible for something like that."

"Don't worry, Pop, I'm no amateur. It won't come to that."

I took a big swig of water and glanced at my phone. I still had plenty of time before I needed to get to the Twilight and start setting up for the movie. A leisurely morning with my computer would be nice, maybe . . . if it weren't a reminder of how little I actually had to do. How little I actually had in the world.

Still, though . . . I was looking forward to road-tripping with Archie. I almost didn't want to admit to myself how much I was looking forward to that. Especially since my phone was registering exactly zero missed calls or texts.

"Have you . . ." I tried to sound casual, but maybe Pop was right, and I really was biting off more than I could chew, because my throat caught for a second there. I pulled it together. "Have you seen Archie in here lately, Pop?"

Has it really been a week since we talked like nothing ever changed?

It had. Of course it had. And I knew it.

He stared off for a second, thinking it over. "Lately? I don't know about that. Sometimes he does lunch runs for his father—he's a good boy, that one."

A good boy, that was Archie Andrews. A good friend, too—or, at least, he used to be.

"But, no," Pop said, breaking into my momentary reverie. "I haven't seen him in a few days at least. I don't know what he's been getting up to. Last time he sat down he was with you—the night of the storm. A week ago?"

"Right." The night he told me about his music, when we made the Centerville plan.

"Shouldn't *I* be asking *you* what he's up to?" Pop went on. "You two being so inseparable?" He was playing casual, but I knew he was taking in every word, every micro-expression. Pop doesn't miss a thing.

"Things change, I guess," I said, finally admitting the unavoidable aloud. "Even in sleepy old Riverdale."

The door chimed as if on cue, so perfectly timed, for a second I thought we'd somehow conjured Archie up with the sheer power of suggestion. But it was Dilton Doiley, fresh from whatever psycho-survivalist predawn scenario he'd been rehearsing with his Adventure Scouts.

"Now, *there's* your 'predictable.'" I arched an eyebrow. Dilton took the whole "be prepared" adage to the next level.

Dilton scowled at me and adjusted his red bandana

(though, to be fair, his default expression is pretty intense and scowl-ish).

He pushed a hank of thick hair out of glasses-framed eyes. "It's crucial to be ready for any and all possible contingencies in today's fraught climate, Jughead. We don't all have the luxury of burying ourselves in"—he waved a hand at my laptop—"make-believe *stories*."

"Sure, okay," I said, not wanting to get Dilton more riled up. "Fraught climate, whatever. Silly me, here I was, just calling Riverdale 'sleepy.'" I shrugged. "No drama here." *Unless you count whatever's going on with Archie.* "I mean, except for that time you got called out by Weatherbee for having a . . . was it a knife at school?" That was May, just before finals.

More scowling. "A pocketknife, yes. Standard Scout-issue. The whole thing was ridiculous. But such is my burden." He nodded, like he was reassuring himself of what he was saying. "You have no idea what it's like, Jughead. Knowing something horrible is going to happen. Being *certain*. But not knowing what or when."

"Dilton, did anyone ever tell you, you can be kind of a downer?" I smiled to show I was teasing. (I mean, people tell *me* that all the time. Takes one to know one, and all.)

"My dad always said, 'The world is tough and unforgiving. The universe is out to get us. Everything *doesn't* always work out for the best.'"

I thought of my mom, of Jellybean's face peering back over her shoulder, out the window of the backseat of Mom's car as they drove off. "Fair enough."

"Just look around," he went on, as if there were some clue to the mysteries of the unknown etched into the linoleum surface of Pop's countertop. "Don't you think it's . . . *significant* that the holiday overlaps with a *blood moon*?"

"I . . . gotta be honest, I didn't realize it did." *And I have no idea what a 'blood moon' is*, I didn't bother to add. "Dilt . . . didn't Weatherbee tell you to maybe, uh, relax a little?" Between the laser beams burning from his eyes and the odd vibe Jason Blossom was throwing off in the parking lot, the air at Pop's was seriously strange today.

He snorted. "What does he know? An ostrich, like the rest of them—keeps his head buried in the sand. The apocalypse is nigh. And my Scouts and I, we're going to be ready."

"If the apocalypse is so *nigh*, why are you dragging a bunch of Adventure Scouts into the woods to greet it with open arms?"

"You're not following me, Jones. *I'm* the only one who's prepared for it. My dad trained me. And the boys need me."

"Okay, okay." I should've known better than to try to reason with Dilton. "I'll keep an eye out for this blood moon you speak of. It'll probably be the most exciting thing to happen to Riverdale in a long time."

"Be careful what you wish for, son," Pop chimed in. "You may think this town is sleepy, but you're young still. Dilton may be a touch wound-up, but I wouldn't count him out."

"Thank you." Dilton sniffed.

"What are you talking about, Pop?" Talk about Spidey-sense; my skin was tingling the way it does when I'm on a good story thread, when the words are pouring out of my fingers on their own.

"We do have some history. Riverdale—and also the Chock'Lit Shoppe. Keep in mind, Pop's has been here even longer than Riverdale itself. Of course, it was different in those days."

My ears perked up and my fingers crept toward my laptop. Something told me this was going to be worth recording. I glanced at Pop, expectant. Dilton perched himself on the stool beside me, just as curious as I was.

"My father, Pop Senior, opened this place as a pharmacy and soda fountain. No food, just ice cream and soda pop."

"No burgers?" My stomach grumbled just thinking about it. "That's a travesty."

"It didn't seem to bother people," Pop said. "I've served all types. Even some celebrities."

"Celebrities. In *Riverdale*?" Josie and her Pussycats were the closest thing we had to celebrities, these days. Thornton Wilder couldn't have written Riverdale more picturesque.

"Sure. We've had the honor of serving some presidents, even, over the years. Some on the campaign trail. Others during . . . less happy times." His eyes darkened for a moment, but he didn't elaborate.

"Neil Armstrong stopped in for a tuna melt once! Guy tracked mud all over my floor," he mused. "Not that I cared, mind you. Those were feet that had touched the moon. Oh, and one night, around two in the morning, that wacky singer . . . Madonna—she rolled in on a party bus with her dancers. She liked my chicken and waffles so much, she offered me tickets to her concert. But I gave 'em to my waitresses. I'm not much for loud events."

"I guess that must've been before she went all macrobiotic," I said. "Pop, those are some *really* big sightings." It was crazy that he had all these stories just locked up inside himself. Maybe when the school year started, I'd think about publishing a profile in *The Blue & Gold* or something. Pop was a local hero, an oral historian.

Then again, publishing in the school newspaper meant *joining* the school newspaper, and as I think I've already established, I'm not much of a joiner. So maybe not . . .

"You're darn right those are big sightings." Pop was clearly proud, and rightly so. "Matter of fact, see that dollar bill over there on the wall?" He pointed to a small frame by the register that I'd somehow never noticed before. "That was a tip my father got from one of the most famous . . . or should I say, *infamous* guests we've ever had.

"My father had just opened the shop a couple of years prior. It was a Tuesday, during the middle of the afternoon rush. There was electricity in the air. You know how you can feel it?"

"Yes," I said at the same time Dilton said, "Definitely." *Kinda feeling it now, Pop, to be honest.*

"A strange couple came in."

Hmm. "Strange, how?"

"My father said after, he could tell immediately they weren't from around here. Their clothes, their Texas accents . . . obvious stuff, really. But it was more than that. Some people . . . they have the whiff of death about them."

"Yup." Dilton sighed, but I waved a hand to shush him so I wouldn't miss a word.

"These two, they reeked of it," Pop said. "It wafted in with them. They sat too close, laughed too loud—couldn't keep their hands off each other."

"Sounds like typical Riverdale High students to me," I joked.

Pop looked at me sternly. "My father told me, that day, he saw something that chilled him to the marrow. He went to give that couple their tab and it was like . . . he had a vision, a glimpse of some future." Pop shook his head. "Whatever he saw, those two would meet a bad end."

"Violence? Your father had a premonition?" Were we talking about ESP, here? That was maybe too much, even for a storyteller like me.

"He didn't go into too much detail, but yes. A shootout. And a bad end. My father wasn't psychic or anything like that—this wasn't some usual event for him. It hadn't happened before, and as far as I know, it never happened again." Pop swallowed. "The fella gave my father five dollars. Whole bill was only eighty cents. This was during the depression, mind you, and most folks were hard up. But not Bonnie Parker and Clyde Barrow."

"Hold up—you're telling me your father waited on *Bonnie and Clyde*?" That electric charge zipped down my spine. I couldn't type fast enough.

"I'm telling you exactly that, son."

"I guess I was wrong," I admitted. "Maybe there's more to Riverdale than meets the eye. Maybe there always has been." Here I'd been thinking milk shakes and manicured lawns. But gangsters and gun molls lurked, too.

Dilton rolled his eyes. "No duh. And knowledge is power. You're from the Southside, Jug. I don't know why it's so hard for you to believe Riverdale could have layers."

I bristled at the mention of class warfare. Sure, my father had a Serpent jacket hanging on a hook behind the trailer door. But he was a Serpent in name only. This wasn't some

West Side Story, Jets versus Sharks thing. "Maybe I should get myself one of those pocketknives."

"Joke all you want. If Pop and I can't convince you, you'll have to learn the hard way." He spoke with no inflection. It almost sounded like a threat.

"Dilton, you really need to chill by, like, at least ten percent. Next you'll be telling me that Sweetie is real." I couldn't resist adding in a reference to Riverdale's own version of the Loch Ness Monster, a mythical creature that haunts the banks of the Sweetwater River.

"Jughead Jones, you hush," Pop chided. "Maybe Sweetie is real, maybe not . . . but it's no secret we've lost too many to that river. When I was growing up, nearly every summer we'd hear about another kid who got careless or distracted and drowned in the river. Some people accepted it as fact, but *plenty* others believed there was more to the story."

I opened my mouth, then closed it again. Just a minute ago, Pop was telling us his father had presaged the deaths of Bonnie and Clyde, and it had seemed plausible enough. Now he was saying the river—our town, even—was innately cursed.

"I, uh . . ." The conversation was veering on fantastical . . . but the air in the diner still had that electric feeling Pop spoke of. That sense that we were on the verge of something ineffable.

Something we wouldn't be able to control. And we wouldn't be able to take back, either.

Dilton smirked at me. I guess it's always a treat when the resident wiseass runs out of comebacks.

"Sure," I said, snapping my laptop shut and standing. "More to the story."

"Blood moon, Jughead," Dilton said, his tone singsongy and suggestive. "Let me know if you need . . . anything. The Scouts and I are watching."

"That's . . . reassuring." I nodded at Pop, our shorthand for *We'll deal with the bill later*. (Speaking of mythical—was anything more mythical than this ongoing *later* we dealt in?) I started to say my good-byes, when I heard it:

The spiky, stuttering roar of an engine.

A *motorcycle* engine.

There was only one bike around town that made that kind of a racket: my father's.

But what the hell would he be doing here now?

I ran to the door just in time to see a bike tearing off in the distance—a cloud of exhaust trailing from the tailpipe that was as familiar a sight to me as Mom's famous boxed mac and cheese.

Dad. Definitely Dad.

The bike was familiar, yeah. And so was the Serpent insignia on the back of his jacket as he drove away.

71

Dad:

Jason, you will respond to these texts. I know you've seen Cheryl. I know you're receiving these. I need to know that you're on board.

Dad:

This is not a joke, young man. I have expectations. We all do. You have a duty to your family. You are a Blossom.

Dad:

Jason, there will be consequences for your disobedience.

∿∿∿

Dad:

Stay put. The snake is on the way.

Jason:

He's late and people are wondering why I'm here so early. Looks weird.

Dad:

Just do as you're told.

Jason:

U having second thoughts?

Polly:

Never. Just wish I could talk to Betty before I go. Even if I can't tell her the whole truth.

Jason:

We can't tell anyone the whole truth. But keep trying B. Tomorrow morning is still a while away.

Polly:

I know! Feels like it will never come.

Jason:

It will. & then we'll be together . . . & free.

Polly:

73

CHAPTER SEVEN

VERONICA

"You are a radiant goddess!" A willowy blonde shrieked at me with an intensity that was totally at odds with her cool, lithe, flawlessly fit presentation.

Radiant goddesses don't usually grunt and drip with sweat, but all bets are off during spin class, and I was in the zone. Besides, there was no one around to see me in all my red-faced, effortful, demigod glory, anyway: SoulCycle was *so* 2015, and switching to Flywheel when the owners parted ways felt like throwing down in a very East Coast/West Coast fashion. When it comes to taking sides, at the end of the day, I'm always going to be #TeamMe.

So what's a girl to do for her daily burn? Simple, obvi: If you build it, they will come. The *it* being a three-bike Peloton studio off my bedroom (we renovated the screening room after buying the apartment below us, converting the two, and creating a brand-new screening room with twice the seating. Win-win!). The *they* being Heather (and sometimes, Oceanna, when Heather is doing a pre-awards-show stint with her celeb clients in LA). Mom found her at the peak of Orangetheory madness on the Upper West Side; she poached her into private-client work, and Heather's never looked back since.

Heather reached for a set of hand weights stashed behind the seat of her bike and raised an eyebrow, indicating that I should do the same. I gave her my fiercest glare.

"Almost there," she urged. "And triceps are the new core."

I wished we could just fast-forward to whatever the new triceps would inevitably be, but I managed to squeeze out two sets of reps before the music slowed to some half-time, ballad-remix version of a popular club jam, Heather dimmed the lights, and she finally muttered those magic words: "Unclip."

"*You* are a radiant goddess," I told her, happily dismounting the bike and stretching one leg across the handlebars to release my screaming hamstrings. "Sorry for the things I may have said during hill climbs."

"Great work today, Ronnie. As usual." Heather smiled.

"You know me. I'm an overachiever." I freed my hair from its messy ponytail and shook it out, letting the tension in my neck and shoulders go.

"No wonder you can be so intimidating."

I turned to see Old Faithful—aka Nick St. Clair—standing just beyond the propped-open doorway of the studio. Nick is the quintessential uptown boy—think Gatsby in high school, for better or for worse. And he was essentially wrapped around my perfectly manicured finger. But he still couldn't resist an appreciative once-over of my form-fitting workout clothes. (And really, I couldn't blame him. Lycra works for me.)

"Don't leer, it's unbecoming of a man of your station," I teased. "And don't pretend you're scared of me."

(He wasn't pretending. Everyone is at least a little bit scared of me. How else would I ever get anything done?)

"Smithers let me in. He sent me up with this." Nick held out a small silver tray with two glasses of cucumber-infused water. I took one gratefully and passed the other to Heather.

Heather took a sip, then leaned in to give me a sweaty air kiss on the cheek. She patted my shoulder. "Same time next week. Keep it tight, doll. You've got resistance bands if you want to stay on top of those triceps."

"*If.*" I laughed and watched Nick watch Heather as she bounced out of the house in her own similarly tight spin clothes.

I jostled him. "Leering again."

"Sorry." He turned back to me and gave me his full attention. "Of course, I only have leer for you. *I'll* stay on top of those triceps if you want me to."

"Ew. Be still my heart. Chivalry is not dead." It wasn't *Casablanca*—more like the first act of an Apatow movie—but believe it or not, for Nick St. Clair, that was actually a stab at *romantic*.

We made our way back upstairs, where the dining room table had become command central: Mom was there, of course, alongside Rafe, in his signature uniform of black skinny jeans, gray V-neck, and leather Gucci high-tops. His Bluetooth earpiece winked from behind one ear, and he was fixated on an iPad with a level of concentration that verged on superhuman. Various other white-suited helpers flitted around the space, arranging artful sprays of lush, long-stemmed flowers, stringing elegant, dainty fairy lights, and clustering the furniture for optimal mingling capacity. They were the literal pros at this; my parents and I, we were old pros. I had to hand it to my mother, we had practically as many people in our house right now as we would have guests later, in various stages of event preparation, and she didn't have a single raven-hued lock out of place. Her lipstick—NARS, Natalie—was impeccable. The woman was frazzle-proof.

"Coming along nicely, Mom," I said, eyeing a giant bowl filled with gold-plated sand dollars.

"Sotheby's," Mom said, catching my gaze. "From Douglas Fairbanks's Palm Beach estate."

"That's a mega score," I said, admiring the display. "And they'll look amazing in the—"

"Master bath vanity at Lodgehampton!" we finished together, laughing.

Rafe glanced at us, holding up a finger to say we should keep it down. We giggled, but more quietly now, chastened. Finally finished with his call, he set the iPad down, back to the IRL world.

"Ladies, you're adorable, but you're giving uptown dysfunctional families a bad name."

"Give it up, Rafe—the Lodges are actually a happy family. I know, it's like finding a unicorn in your backyard. Very unexpected, and even more unbelievable." Nick sounded wistful for a minute, even though his life was pretty charmed, too, I knew. But he was right—Mom and Dad were devoted to each other, and both were totally devoted to me. It may have made me easy to hate, among other, less fortunate peers, but what did I care? My life was damn near perfect.

"You say that like you're Oliver Twist and not Jay Gatsby," I teased.

"I feel like you're missing the point of that book."

"I'm really not." I smirked.

"Play nice, *m'hija*," Mom interrupted. She smiled at Nick.

"And speaking of happy families, we're looking forward to seeing your parents tonight."

"They can't wait. Everyone knows the Fourth with the Lodges is the event of the summer."

"Is that why you're here at the crack of"—I checked my Apple Watch (Daddy bought me my Cartier when I started high school, but sometimes, you want a statement piece that *also* sends texts)—"well, the crack of noon, I suppose, so a civilized hour. Barely." Honestly, I'd been up since 7 a.m. with all the activity swirling around me, but weren't teenage boys supposed to be nocturnal?

"Aren't you happy to see me?" Nick fake-pouted. It had been a while, actually; Nick and his family generally fled to the Italian Riviera in the weeks after school let out, some palazzo in Sardinia, while the rest of us fought to the death for a parking space at Nick and Toni's in the East End like fools. He'd picked up a tan there, a slight flush to his chiseled cheekbones that actually went a long way toward forgiving an early and unannounced arrival.

"Always happy to see you, *mon cherie*. But still surprised."

"She meant to say, she's busy," Mom put in. "Ronnie, we need your unassailable good taste while we get the house in order."

"By 'unassailable good taste' she means 'extra set of hands,'" I assured Nick. "It's her polite way of moving us along."

"Those are your words, not mine," Mom protested, "but Rafe does have a checklist of action items just for you."

Rafe tapped the screen of his iPad meaningfully. "Some phone calls," he explained.

"I'm sorry, Nick, it's total chaos. Maybe we can get some quality time at the party?" I made a face; we both knew it wasn't likely I'd have *more* time with him when hostess duties kicked in for real.

"Walk me to the door?" I would have done it anyway, but his eyebrows pinched together in a way that told me he'd come to discuss something specific.

Once there, he turned to me, shifting his weight. Something was definitely up with my boy.

"What is it, Nicky? What on earth has the unflappable Nick St. Clair sweating?"

He flushed. "It's just . . . Ah, I don't really know how to say this, Ronnie."

"Say what?" I reached to brush his hair back from his forehead and he flinched slightly and pulled back from my hand.

"Okay," I said slowly. I ticked off the facts on my fingers as I spoke. "I haven't seen you in weeks, you come by to say hi, I reach out to touch you, and you shrink away from me. What am I missing? Is this like some kind of riddle? Does it start with a block of ice and a locked room?" I reached those fingers out in a threatening tickle gesture, prompting a half-smile.

"Ronnie, stop. Sorry, I'm being super weird," Nick said, looking more and more sheepish. "I need to just come out with it."

"With this much buildup, I hope we're looking at a *Dynasty*—the original—level of dramatic twist."

(Who doesn't love some prime Joan Collins?)

"The thing is, yeah, I've been gone a few weeks and, I mean . . . well, you know I have a reputation of, um, let's say, *dating around*."

"You do have a well-established reputation as an unrepentant ladies' man," I agreed. "Hard-earned."

"But, well . . . while I was gone, I realized . . . Well, I realized I was thinking a lot. I was thinking a lot about *you*, Veronica."

Oh. My. God.

"Nick St. Clair," I said, shocked, but pleasantly so. "What's happening here? Are you here to formally court me? Ask me on an honest-to-Gucci date-date? Because if so, that's charming. Amazingly retro." If Nick was having bona fide feels for me, I wasn't sure what our next step was. But it wasn't terrible news.

"In a good way?"

I laughed. "Yes, silly! But you know, you could have just come right out and told me."

"I tried! Like I said, you can sometimes be intimidating." He pinched his fingers together in that "just a smidge" motion.

"*Moi*? I don't believe it." I swatted his smidge away.

"Believe it." He gazed at me, steadily now, locking eyes with mine. "Anyway. It probably sounds kind of douchey to say, but you've known me forever, so I'll just be straight: I honestly never expected there was a girl who'd stay on my mind for weeks at a time, even when we were apart."

"So this is some kind of romantic record for you?"

Nick nodded. "So, I guess the only question mark here is you."

"Meaning, a date-date," I said. "Even though we've never done more than flirt."

"A date-date. Exactly. Think full-on Julia Roberts movie." Nick bit his lip.

He suddenly seemed very young and *very* vulnerable, neither of which I was used to. It was a little bit thrilling, to be honest, being able to reduce Nick to such insecurity. But it wasn't his most irresistible moment.

What can I say? I'm attracted to power. It's a Lodge thing.

The dusting of freckles he'd acquired in Sardinia quivered high against his cheekbones. Poor boy; I had to give him some kind of response.

"Nick," I started, giving the hand that was still in mine a squeeze, "you know I adore you."

"But . . . maybe not in a 'that' type of way?"

"Honestly?" I swallowed. "I'm not sure. But, maybe that's because I never thought about it before."

"Well, maybe . . . just think about it now. We can do a boat ride in Central Park. Or the Coney Island Cyclone. It will be a date worthy of an eighties rom-com montage." He moved closer to me now, put his hands on my shoulders. I could feel his breath on my cheek, the warmth from his skin. The sensations conspired to confuse me even more; I was glad to have time to think about all of this.

"I'll think. I swear." My skin felt prickly, like before a lightning storm, like I was seeing Nick St. Clair in a new light.

"Take your time," Nick said, his voice husky. "But not *too* much time."

"It's a lot to think about," I said, my voice soft.

"It is," Nick said, whispering as well. "I should probably go so you can get started." He pulled me to him so his lips just brushed my cheek. "See you at the party?"

"What?" For a second I was practically hypnotized. Me: Veronica Lodge, who had everyone in my life eating out of the palm of my hand. "Um, of course. The party." Suddenly, I was looking forward to it even more. I hadn't thought that was possible.

Nick gave a wave and disappeared into the elevator. I shook my head to try to clear away the spontaneous burst of oxytocin. I had phone calls to make! And other action items to see about. I couldn't afford to be in a fog all day. Not even one as unexpected and delicious as this.

I turned to head back to the dining room and nearly collided with Smithers. He had a dauntingly tall stack of papers in his arms, Lodge Industries letterhead winking out from the top of the pile. He seemed startled when he realized he'd bumped into me.

"Doing a little light filing, Smithers?" I joked. "How have you managed to escape party planning duties? I'd been given to believe it was an all-hands-on-deck situation."

Smithers smiled, but—and it may have been my imagination—the expression looked strained, especially around his eyes. "Yes, well. Not to worry, Miss Veronica, I'll be joining you just as soon as I finish disposing of these."

"Recycling is that way," I reminded him, pointing toward the various trash chutes built into the wall off our eat-in kitchen. So odd; Smithers was older, but not *senile*-older.

"Of course," Smithers said. But he continued on in the opposite direction—toward Daddy's study.

It didn't make a lot of sense, but it also didn't exactly worry me. Honestly, with the party tonight and Nick's visit, I had more than enough on my mind, as it was.

∿∿∿

Midge:

Moose, we on for Twilight tonight? Any chance u can get away earlier?

Midge:

Don't leave me hanging, Moose!

Midge:

KK u must be super busy. ttyl & hopefully c u 2! 😊

CHAPTER EIGHT

ARCHIE

From Geraldine's, I had two quick stops to make—and all before Dad realized I was even gone. He believed me when I told him I went running—mostly because I did, most mornings; Coach Clayton made it *very* clear we had to keep in shape over the summer—but it was still better not to be noticed in the first place.

Even if I did hate keeping things from Dad.

First up was Riverdale High. The tall, redbrick building looked just like the first Google image you'd find if you searched "typical American high school," with a wide, curving staircase and bright red painted front doors. Those doors are locked in the summer unless there's a special event going on. Mostly.

But the back entrance, out by the football field? That one always stays open.

It's one of Weatherbee's worst-kept "secrets." Coach Clayton holds drills toward the end of summer as we get closer to the first day of school, and he wants his team to have access to the gym for practice and training, even if we're gonna do it on our own. So it started as a perk reserved for Bulldogs. But this is a small town, and everyone knows everyone else's business—for the most part—so of course, students know how to get in if they need to. And more than a few take advantage of that, now and then.

The good news is, there aren't a lot of students trying to get *into* school over summer vacation. So my own secrets were safe for that much longer.

It's easy to joke that Ms. Grundy—I mean *Geraldine*—is, you know, *teaching me music*, like, with the sarcastic quote marks and everything. But like I said, she *is*, and we wouldn't even . . . well, we wouldn't even be doing anything in the first place if it weren't for the music. She's the one person in the world I trust with my songwriting. And she's the one person in the world who takes it seriously. Who takes *me* seriously.

So anyway, Ms. Grundy had said there was some blank sheet music in her desk in the music room, and I was going to grab some so we could bring it with us when we went camping. Geraldine says you never know when and where inspiration will strike. She tends to be right about these kinds of things. So out in nature, with her at my side . . . it seemed pretty likely I could get inspired. I mean, just Geraldine her-self for sure had that effect on me.

The halls were dim, even though the sun was up by now. It wasn't the first time I'd been in the school after hours (or did summer vacation count as *before*?), but it was still a little eerie how quiet and still everything was, like someone watching over us had pressed "pause" on a giant remote. The music room, too, was completely empty, with no signs that anyone was *ever* there except for Josie and her crew's setup. They sometimes rehearsed here. (Like the Bulldogs, the Pussycats have privileges of their own. Look, no one ever said high school was a totally even playing field. Even if it bothers me, there's not a whole lot I can do about it.)

I found the sheet music easily—it was in the top drawer of her desk, along with some different-colored sticky-note pads, and a pot of lip stuff that looked fancy-ish, like it didn't come from the drugstore. The label said "rose," and I made a note of it: She liked roses. Like, just in case there was ever a time when I would bring her flowers. This could be some kind of clue, something to tell me what she preferred.

I don't know, thinking like that got my stomach twisted up. I mean, I couldn't imagine a future time without . . . me and Geraldine. But I'm not dumb, either. She's my *teacher*. I couldn't exactly see where this was all going to end. Or maybe I *could* see it . . . but I didn't want to.

I shut the drawer and closed the door on those thoughts, too, for now.

With the sheet music safe in my backpack, I made sure to leave the room exactly the same as I found it, scooting one or two chairs I'd jostled back into place. I was deep in my own head, in my thoughts, when I walked back out into the hallway . . .

. . . and smack into Cheryl Blossom.

She looked as startled as I was, and dropped whatever she was carrying, but she recovered quickly. That was Cheryl for you. She has reflexes like a cat. And she'll scratch if you catch her off-guard.

"Archie Andrews," she said, flipping her perfectly waved red hair over one shoulder. "Aren't you the stealthy one. What brings you to the hallowed halls of Riverdale High so early on this picturesque summer morning?"

"I, uh, left something in my locker," I said. It was the first thing that came to my mind. It was none of Cheryl's business why I was here, of course. But that wouldn't stop her.

"Hmm." She pursed her bright red lips together. "A likely story. Except, you were coming from the music room. Your locker is down the south hall. So, I'm thinking, you must have ulterior motives." She tapped a fingernail—also cherry-red—against her chin like she was turning it over in her head.

"Cheryl, calm down," I told her. "Not everyone is always scheming like you are." If only she could hear my heart thudding in my chest. So far, no one knew about Geraldine and me—and we were going to keep it that way, no matter what.

"Touché," she said, bending down to pick up what she'd been carrying. "Fair enough, even if thou doth protest just a wee bit too much. Aren't you the good boy, always giving the general public the benefit of the proverbial doubt?"

Good boy. People liked to say that about me. I wondered what Cheryl would think if she knew the truth—if everyone knew—about who I really am. Lying to my father, second-guessing Coach . . . and, of course, Geraldine . . .

"Wait, you've got . . . Jason's varsity jacket?" I didn't even mean to pry—I wasn't exactly in the best position to snoop, even if I wanted to—it just came out when I realized what she had in her arms.

"So observant." Her voice was defiant enough, but . . . Was it me, or did the slightest hint of guilt cross *her* face, now?

I didn't know what Cheryl had to feel guilty about.

But I didn't know why she'd need that jacket, either. She and Jason were so close they were practically conjoined, but still.

"Just doing a favor for Jay-Jay," she said, reading the expression on my face. "He needs it now, god knows why, and he's busy with . . . well, let's just say my darling brother has quite a lot on his to-do list today. So hashtag *twinning* to the rescue."

It still felt like she was hiding something, but I had to hand it to her: She was a master of spin. And I wasn't going to push things. Not when I had my own to-do list for the day to take care of.

She fixed her deep brown eyes on mine. "Family is everything, Archiekins."

"I agree," I said, a little shaken by how intense she was. I mean, *intense* is basically Cheryl's default mode. But still. "Actually, speaking of family, I've gotta get to Pop's. I was going to pick up some coffee and some breakfast for Dad and some of the crew."

"Funny, I'm just coming from there. It was practically hopping, given the predawn hour. You just missed your own surrogate brother—and his father, too, for that matter. Though I don't think their paths even crossed."

"Jughead was at Pop's?" I don't know why I was surprised; Jug practically lives at Pop's. I felt a twinge of guilt; I didn't know all the details, but I knew things weren't great for Jug at home, these days. And I knew that once upon a time, I *would* have known all the details. And didn't we have a plan or something for the holiday? Shoot, I'd forgotten all about that once Geraldine and I started making plans of our own. I'd have to text him soon. Just one more way the "good guy" was falling down on the job lately.

Then the rest of what she'd said hit me. "*FP* was at Pop's earlier?" Jughead's dad wasn't exactly known for being an early riser. More like the textbook definition of a night owl.

Cheryl shrugged. "I heard a motorcycle; I saw a jacket. I didn't exactly stop to investigate. I was only there to touch base with Jay-Jay. I was preoccupied; it was quick. Anyway, doesn't he work for your dad?"

"Yeah." FP and my father had started what was now Andrews Construction together as partners. These days, FP was part of the crew. Dad had never given me the full story on that.

Maybe he and I keep more from each other than I liked to think.

Cheryl's phone blared, interrupting us. (Blondie's "Rip Her to Shreds" was her ringtone—the choice was so incredibly Cheryl, I wanted to laugh, but the look on her face when she saw the caller ID stopped me.) Cheryl didn't bother to do more than toss a wave over her shoulder as she went searching for, I assumed, a more private place to talk. The hallway threw echoes like Moose Mason throws a perfect spiral.

It felt like football was always lurking at the back of my mind—that moment that I knew would come just as soon as practice started up again, that moment where suddenly my music would become public—because it would be a conflict. A distraction. I hated thinking about that moment. But I couldn't *stop* thinking about it.

And then I was leaving again, out the back door, same as I'd come in, out by the—you guessed it—football field, so it really felt like that part of me was something I'd never, ever forget.

(It wasn't that I *wanted* to forget it, not completely. More like I was tired of football being the one thing that defined me. And I was more than tired of feeling like I personally had no say in the matter at all.)

But—Riverdale is a typical *American* town, and there's no forgetting high school football in a typical American town. Not high school football rivalries, either. So the first thing I noticed when I walked outside—the sun blazing overhead in full now—was our field. Our wide green field, the one I knew so well I could practically recognize every blade of grass on the turf from touch alone.

Someone had covered the field in plastic forks.

White plastic forks poked handle-side-up into the air all across the field, spread in two-inch rows like tiny plastic soldiers. It was *insane*. I blinked to be sure I wasn't seeing things.

(I wasn't.)

It must've taken hours to stick these into the field so precisely.

It would take *hours* to pull them out again.

I knew, right away, who was responsible. There was only one group that could be: the Baxter High Ravens, aka the Riverdale Bulldogs' number-one rivals.

My heart sank, staring out at those rows of forks. The Ravens sure were organized. And thorough. When Coach Clayton found out about this, it would be all hands on deck to clear the field. We'd all be recruited. And when Reggie heard about this? It would be all hands on deck to devise a retaliation prank against the Ravens. We'd all be recruited for that, too.

But truth was, I just didn't have the time—or the interest—in either of those things.

Maybe "good guy" Archie would have let Coach know about the field right away. Maybe he would have clued everyone in, acted like a real, literal "team player."

So maybe this was proof that I was getting further and further from being the "good guy" I thought I'd always been. Because I wasn't going to do that. Not if it meant being forced to deal with the fallout so soon.

I didn't even know myself anymore.

I was so spun out thinking about the field and my dad and the secrets it felt like we were all keeping from each other, I almost didn't notice the second thing going on outside. At the edges of the field, where the bleachers came up against the scoreboard . . .

Somebody—some*bodies*—were moving out there.

Maybe I was seeing things, maybe I was too caught up in the millions of thoughts elbowing for space in my own brain. But it looked like . . . Kevin Keller was out there, leaning against the aluminum struts? It definitely looked like Kevin. And he definitely wasn't alone.

Does Kevin have a boyfriend? I didn't think so, but there was someone else out there. Someone else I thought I recognized. I mean, the guy who was with him was pretty recognizable.

You'd have to be, with a name like *Moose*.

From: JJBlossom@MapleFarm.net
To: BombshellC@MapleFarm.net
Re: Sister

I needed to write, to leave a note and thank you, again, for all your help in planning my escape. You speak of our "twintuition," and yes, we know each other's minds almost as well as we each know our own, but you can't imagine how much your steadfast support has meant to me during these endless, stressful stretches of scheming, plotting, and preparing.

I couldn't leave without a proper good-bye, one that would hopefully paint a fuller, truer picture of why, exactly, it is that escape feels like my sole remaining option.

You've been frank in your disapproval of my relationship with Polly; you're not the only one. If only you knew how much your displeasure affected me—so much more painful than Mother and Father's rejection. Perhaps your reasons for distrusting Polly were purer than theirs? I can only speculate—perhaps the way she encroached on my affections, my priorities, was stressful for you.

But sister, I deceived you. I suppose we can't know everything about each other; you didn't realize that my breakup with Polly was only a ruse. One we can't maintain any longer . . .

[DELETE]

PART II: AFTERNOON

NOTICE OF INTENT TO FORECLOSE

(Mortgage Loan Default)

Date of Notice: June 30

Name of Borrower(s): Manfred Muggs, Sr.

THIRD AND FINAL NOTICE

This Notice is Required by Rockland County Law (Real Property Article, S7-105.1(a), Annotated Code of Rockland County).

You are at risk of losing the property described in this Notice to foreclosure. You are in default on your mortgage loan and if you do not pay what is owed, or otherwise cure your default, or enter into a loss mitigation agreement with us (such as a loan modification or other loss mitigation program) we may file a foreclosure action against the property upon the later of 45 days after we sent this notice to you or 90 days after your default.

You may be eligible for certain programs to avoid foreclosure, but you must submit the enclosed Loss Mitigation Application and required documents to your lender or servicer.

To obtain the exact amount needed to bring your loan current and cure this default, please call us at the toll-free telephone number. **If you are unable to cure the default, please contact us immediately to discuss loan repayment options or other possible foreclosure avoidance options, or you may fill out the enclosed Loss Mitigation Application and send it to us along with the required documents in (or at the address on) the preprinted envelope provided.**

HAVE A NICE DAY!

CHAPTER NINE

BETTY

WOOD WORKS

Guys, we get it: Whether it's your bedroom, your dorm room, or your very first big-girl apartment, your personal space is your number-one place to express yourself. But if you're not an honest-to-Gaia homeowner (and who among us is? #GOALS), your options for personal expression may be limited.

But here at *Hello Giggles*, we don't believe in limits!

That's where temporary wallpaper comes in.

I know, I know, we've been talking about wallpaper for a few years now; you're thinking, by this point florals are *so* passé.

WE AGREE.

Woodworking and wood details are the next big thing.

And the key to achieving the look on a young-thang-on-the-go's budget?

Again we say: wallpaper.

Confused? Stay with us now.

Believe it or not, this season's patterns are industrial, earthy, and decidedly unlike your grandmother's latticework and chintz florals. Can you say *beadboard* or *wainscot*? Because that's just what's on-trend and in stores right now.

It's wallpaper. It's wood. It's two looks in one, for one unbeatable style statement. And it's yours, all yours.

You're welcome.

Dear Diary:

I'd run out of ways to say wallpaper and woodworking puns that weren't borderline PG-13, but after a working lunch, some blood, sweat, and tears (and caffeine!), my first piece for *Hello Giggles* was officially filed and in the proverbial bag. I didn't know if I wanted to do a touchdown dance or collapse in a puddle under my desk from exhaustion. Possibly both.

(But not at the same time. That sounded tiring.)

No, it wasn't Pulitzer material. It was barely even *People* magazine material. Maybe a notch above *Us Weekly* if I was being generous with myself. It was temporary wallpaper, over and over again. But there it was, my name, Elizabeth Cooper, as a proper byline. And that meant something.

No—it meant everything.

I sighed, exhausted and satisfied (curling up under my desk was looking more and more appealing). I loosened my ponytail for a moment, rolling my neck out and thinking about the piece on Veronica Lodge still left to write. *Miles to go.* She hadn't responded to any of my texts or calls. I strongly doubted email was going to be the winning effort. Was I supposed to Twitter-stalk her or "slide into her DMs?" That seemed . . . unprofessional. And very not me. Not even LA me.

My phone buzzed against my desk, the alert making it jump. Polly again.

Sis! the message read. *Leaving me hanging!* The urgency behind her words was real. But I was fried . . . and also crazed—the worst possible combination.

I grabbed my phone. *Sorry! Busy day! 1st (and 2nd) assignment/s! Talk later?* I knew Polly'd appreciate me getting a crack at a byline. She knew how much that meant to me.

There was the briefest of pauses before the phone buzzed again. *OMG! So huge! SO excited for you! Promise you won't forget me when you're a famous author.*

I knew she'd get it.

Duh, I typed. *Sisters forever. Couldn't forget you if I tried, wouldn't want to.*

She Bitmoji'd me a thumbs-up, blond and smiling like a cheerful anime heroine. *TTYL but PROMISE you'll call TONIGHT.*

I sent my own thumbs-up back. (I've always been particularly proud of my own Bitmoji's perfect high ponytail.) Normally, I'd never keep Polly waiting—we talk, like, ten times a day, minimum, anyway, but it felt like I was on a roll and I needed to keep rolling, no distractions.

I scrolled through my messages again, then my recent calls, just to be sure. Nothing from Veronica Lodge. And, of course, no email, either. Frustrating.

Then again, I'd managed to squeeze two hundred words out about wallpaper. Veronica Lodge was no match for me.

∿∿∿

All those years I spent holed up in my room reading Nancy Drew mysteries, Mom always nagged and tried to get me out of the house. Studying was one thing—Coopers keep their grades up, keep appearances up, keep their chins up, blah, blah, blah . . . but reading, ugh. Alice Cooper was not impressed.

"Elizabeth, what have I taught you? Boys don't make passes at girls who wear glasses," she'd say, hovering in my doorway.

"Mom, what decade are you living in? No one cares if I read, and if they do, well, forget them! And besides—I don't wear glasses, anyway." I blinked at her like an eager Disney character to emphasize the statement.

Mom rolled her eyes; we both knew that wasn't the point. But she left me alone about the Nancy Drew, in the end. *Finally.*

She tried, anyway, is the point—she wanted a good girl for a daughter, but not necessarily a brainiac. Joke's on her, though, because I read all the time now—and I'm almost a professional writer with this summer internship.

But back to Nancy Drew, my first and longest literary love. I loved reading about a teen girl—*she could be me!* (even though I was, like, ten at the time)—and how with her wits and her friends, she could crack any mystery. I wanted to be just like her.

And now, Diary? I may finally have my chance.

The thing is, nothing mysterious ever happened in Riverdale. (If Halloween candy went "missing" before the trick-or-treaters came, Jughead was usually the culprit.) But based on what just happened at work, I'm wondering if maybe, just maybe, someone's out to get me.

Paranoid? Sure. Crazy? Maybe. But these are the facts:

There I was, flush from the high of filing my first story. A date tonight with a cute boy. An encyclopedic knowledge of temporary wallcoverings that would probably never ever come in handy again, but WHO CARED? I was tired, I was energized, I was exhilarated, my scalp ached from constantly tightening my ponytail out of my face, and I'd never felt better.

Also, I was hungry, I realized.

I left my phone on my desk and made my way to the *Hello Giggles* kitchen. Like everything else in the office, it was decorated in muted, cheery washes of pastel, with gleaming white shelving lining the walls. Taking a cue from trendy tech start-ups, the space was stocked with irresistible "healthy" snacks: coconut water, fresh fruit, dispensers of gourmet nuts and granola, an espresso machine that required a degree in engineering to work, but pumped out a nonfat soy latte better than anything you'd pay for at The Coffee Bean & Tea Leaf.

I grabbed a packet of seaweed chips (I could see Archie laughing, horrified that I was willingly eating things like seaweed and sushi now that I was an LA girl) and an apple, and bounced back to my desk.

When I got there, Rebecca was waiting for me.

I didn't love the look on her face.

"Hey," I said, trying to keep my smile from wavering. She looked upset about something, but what could it possibly have to do with me?

"Betty," she began, dashing any hope I was clinging to that it didn't have to do with me.

"What's up?" I felt dumb, standing there with my snacks, but she was at my desk, blocking it so that I couldn't sit or put anything down, either, so I just had to stand there, awkwardly swinging an apple in one hand and a package of seaweed chips in another.

She put a hand on her hip. "You know at *Hello Giggles* we strive to foster a place of respect."

"Of course." I racked my brain: Had I accidentally disrespected someone? Again, something I thought only happened in old rap videos, but maybe I just didn't know what I didn't know.

"Well." She pursed her lips; I knew from last week's beauty round-up that she was wearing "Up in the air" fly away gloss from the new ColourPop (sic) butterfly-inspired collection.

I mean, if that didn't prove I was Employee of the Freakin' Month, what would?

She hesitated, like she was debating how far to take whatever she was about to say or do. Then she took a deep breath and reached under my desk.

"What are you . . . ?" I trailed off, confused and annoyed, but also not wanting to sound quite as confused and annoyed as I was feeling. Why was she touching my stuff?

She pulled up my backpack, a—you guessed it—floralprinted, quilted nylon number in a pink that had seemed so bright and happy when I saw it in the store, but felt garish and immature and desperately wrong right now. I wanted to cringe, seeing it hanging from Rebecca's perfect, acid-yellow manicured fingers.

Then she put the backpack down on my desk and started rifling through it.

"Okay, what?" Now I stepped forward, outrage outweighing any sense of subservience. But she held a hand up, not physically holding me back—that was probably illegal and very un–*Hello Giggles*, besides—but sending a message loud and clear.

Out it came: a Tarte eye palette in "In Bloom" neutrals. A bronzer and contouring kit. A set of false eyelashes dusted in gold glitter. And then—somehow, the most damning of all—a diaphanous, breezy, cheetah-print maxi dress that I recognized instantly from the Michael Kors resort collection.

(I'm telling you: Employee of the Freakin' Month.)

"Betty." My name coming from Rebecca's mouth sounded like the worst kind of insult.

"I don't know what that is," I started. "I mean, I know what it is, obviously, but I don't know what it's doing in my bag."

"Betty. Stop." That hand again, raised flat to my face, like she couldn't even bear to look me in the eye. "Look, we all know the beauty closet belongs to us all. In fact, it's encouraged that employees play around in there, have fun, try things out. How else will we get our ideas for new stories and features?"

"Right." Although gold false eyelashes would definitely never be my thing, I could say that for sure right now. (Though they do photograph REALLY well. They really make everyone's eyes pop.)

"In fact, I'm pretty sure we've encouraged you to experiment more with the product samples we receive."

That was the truth. Another strike against me. I was kind of a one-and-done girl, even as my LA Betty alter ego: black curling mascara, some lip gloss, a rosy glow. But somehow, I didn't think this was a lecture about my all-too-predictable makeup routine.

"But I didn't think you'd stoop to *this*." Her voice dripped with contempt.

"I didn't. Stoop. But, I guess—" I was babbling, grasping for the right words to undo whatever was happening right now. "Honestly, I'm not even sure what *this* is. I did the sushi run, I've been trying to track down Veronica Lodge, I filed that story about wallpaper . . . that's it. That's literally all I've done today."

"Do you think lying makes this better?" she asked bitterly. "Look, I'm sorry you got caught, and you're embarrassed, but there's no other explanation: At some point, you raided the closet. And that wouldn't be an issue, except that for whatever reason, you decided the top shelf was fair game."

The top shelf: where we put aside anything that's been pulled for a particular feature or upcoming shoot. That was one of the commandments at this place: Thou Shalt Not Pilfer the Top Shelf of the Closet.

I am not, as we know, a rule-breaker by nature.

Of course, I didn't take that stuff.

Anger rose in me, hot and bubbly. I clenched my hands so tightly I could feel little half-moon scars forming where my nails dug into the skin.

"Look, Rebecca," I said, trying to keep my voice from shaking, "I don't know how that stuff got into my bag, but I can promise you, I didn't take it."

She looked doubtful. I couldn't totally blame her: There was the evidence, right in front of us, after all. Seeing is believing. But then that red-hot, live-wire rage bubbled up again: I busted my ass for this place. Every. Damn. Day. Didn't I deserve the benefit of the doubt?

"The question is why, Betty?" Rebecca shoved my backpack back under the desk and gathered all of the "stolen" things up.

"There *is* no why," I said, letting the anger creep into my voice. "I'm telling you, it wasn't me. I know better than to take from the top shelf. And I don't steal. Or lie." I stared at Rebecca, daring her to break eye contact. "You know this internship's been everything I've ever wanted as a writer. You know I've done everything you've asked of me since I got here. Why would I sabotage that? Especially just when you're giving me a big break, a chance to do some writing? Simple: I wouldn't."

She looked away, which I had to admit was a little bit satisfying. Then she looked back, cool and composed even if we still hadn't gotten to the bottom of what was going on. "That stuff ended up in your bag somehow."

"Obviously."

"There's no one else here today, either."

But that wasn't true. The office was empty, but not completely empty.

"There's one person." Cleo was still at the reception desk. She was pretending to idly file her nails, but I could tell from the way her shoulders were thrown back that she was listening to this exchange eagerly.

Nothing like watching a hyena get ripped apart by a lion from your own safe and cozy hiding spot.

"I hope you're not accusing Cleo of somehow setting you up."

I shrugged. "Someone did. I don't know if it was her. All I know is, she's here. And honestly, I don't see why me raising that point is any worse than whatever's being done to me."

There was a long pause, during which I wondered if my time at *Hello Giggles* had just come to a very unceremonious close. And if so, how I'd break that to my friends and family back home in Riverdale, who were all rooting for me.

I tried again, more softly, this time. "Rebecca. I'm not accusing anyone. But it looks like someone *is* setting me up, like you say. I don't know who would do that, or why. Look, I know you don't know me that well, I haven't been here that long, but I *didn't* take that stuff. I wouldn't. Just give me a chance to prove it. And a chance to figure out what's going on."

Rebecca stared at the false eyelashes box like it contained the secrets of the universe. There was another interminable pause, interrupted by little buzzes that had to be Cleo's phone. Ugh, was she *texting* someone about this? I had no idea why she would be out to get me, but the idea that she was savoring it made it all even worse.

Rebecca sighed. "I read your piece, Betty. It was good. You're obviously a natural writer."

She wasn't saying I was forgiven or that this whole thing was over, but it was a compliment. We were heading in the right direction, at least. "Thanks."

"And we believe in second chances at *Hello Giggles.*"

(It was true. Rebecca in particular *loved* a good celebrity comeback story. Rehabilitation with a layer of contrition was her jam. I didn't know what that said about her own backstory.)

"So how about this? Everything goes back into the closet. Top shelf. Not to be disturbed again."

I clenched my fists, wanting to insist again that, of course, I hadn't been the one to disturb it in the first place. But I forced myself to breathe. "Right away."

"Assuming nothing goes missing again—"

Another clench of my fists, another deep breath—

"We'll just chalk this up to an innocent mistake."

But it wasn't MY mistake, I wanted to scream. I knew, though, that it would be the wrong tactic to take.

"Just get the piece on Lodge done and filed," Rebecca said. "I think we're all ready for the holiday to start."

"Done," I said.

And it would be. I'd write that piece on Veronica Lodge, mysterious cipher/heiress about town. And Rebecca would love it.

But that wasn't all. Before I left for the holiday, I'd take care of one other thing:

I was going to Nancy Drew this whole scenario, Diary. I was going to figure out who was working against me.

And then? I was going to shut them down. *Hard.*

FROM THE DESK OF
CLIFFORD C. BLOSSOM

A note to our shareholders:

We at Blossom Maple Farms have heard the recent concerns regarding our efforts to distance our business from its long ties with Lodge Industries, one of our earliest and most controversial partners. Rest assured, our team has conducted extensive research about how best to go about this process, and it will be handled with our signature finesse and fortitude. As you well know, we've worked long and hard to explore the legal ramifications of this decision and don't take these steps lightly.

We at Blossom are fully confident that once this dissolution is complete, our business will see unprecedented growth.

Feel free to reach out to our offices if you have further questions or concerns.

Best,

C Bl—

Blossom Maple Syrup: "Have some syrup with that, Ma'am!"

CHAPTER TEN

JUGHEAD

Next to Pop's, the Twilight might have been my favorite place in Riverdale, even if it weren't the backdrop for the few Norman Rockwell moments I got to have in my freak-show of a life. Even though the Joneses have always been Southsiders—meaning we've never had much cash to spare—there was a time when I spent every Saturday night here, and I wasn't getting paid to work the projector.

These days, it was hard to recall, but there *was* a time when even a screwup, semi-alcoholic, semi-reformed gang member like my dad managed to scrape together enough money to pile the whole family into the car for weekly movie nights.

(Okay, fine, Jellybean was hiding on the floor to save some cash. But it was still pretty decadent for us.)

We'd pack our own snacks from home—off-brand chips, discounted cans of soda way past their expiration date—and once the movie was underway, Jellybean was safe to come out of hiding. (Truth be told, I'm pretty sure the ticket takers always knew she was there and looked the other way. Once in a blue moon, even a Southsider can catch a small break, I guess.) She and I would stretch out in the backseat, propped up on pillows against the doors, and Mom and Dad would hold hands in the front seat. Inside the bubble of that car, there was no fighting. It was some weird, magical alternate universe where somehow, we were granted two-hour increments of being our best selves to one another.

I know, I know—I'm getting uncharacteristically sentimental. But movie nights were those rare occasions where we were all together and happy.

Even before Mom left with Jellybean, it had been a while since Dad arranged one.

So when Sal, the old ticket taker and manager of the Twilight, came to me two years ago and asked if I wanted to take over day-to-day (well, more like night-to-night, but you get it), there wasn't any reason to say no. It wouldn't be spoiling a happy family memory by turning a place of recreation into a place of employment, because by then, those happy memories had already started to fade.

(There's that trademark Jughead Jones cynicism for you.)

Now, yeah, okay, it was work. But it was a relief to have a little bit of pocket change so I could occasionally make a dent in my tab at Pop's. And even with my family having totally unraveled, demolishing any connection the drive-in might have to happy childhood memories, this place was still a haven. *More* so, because now, it was my escape.

I knew the inside of the projection booth as well as I knew the flimsy aluminum walls of our trailer. I'd memorized all the initials carved and Sharpied into them, imagining life histories for those I didn't recognize or personally know. The smell of the field—smoke and stale popcorn, with a hint of deep earth lying just beneath—was almost Pavlovian to me; one whiff and I was relaxed, as close to my happy place as I'd ever be.

My favorite time to be at work was after the movie—which I got to choose, for the most part, and was one of the better perks of the gig—when all the cars had filtered out and the concession stand workers were gone. Then it was just me and the lingering images from the screen, photo negatives replaying in my mind, that satisfied sense of completion hanging in the air.

Setup was okay, too—I loved the metal-on-metal sound the film canisters made when you popped them open, and the whirring of the film being fed into the projector. And even I got a kick out of cheerful, hopeful people up for a fun night out, away from whatever cinematic drama was actually playing out in the movie of their own real lives, ready to be absorbed in someone else's story.

I was pretty absorbed myself, too. The movie was ready to go—a special director's cut edition I'd scored with an alternate ending that would blow everyone's minds—and I was just shoving some clutter out of the way of my seat in the projection booth, idly scanning those walls for my dad's and mom's initials, like I always did. Even knowing that they weren't there, wouldn't suddenly somehow appear from thin air. Knowing that Dad wasn't the type for sentimental gestures of his own, really.

I came outside to clear some trash from the field—the concession guy Ben's job, really, but he wasn't coming in until later, and weirdly, straightening was meditative in a way. As the door banged shut behind me, I saw two figures slouched by the screen. They flinched at the noise and looked up at me, and I realized I knew one of them.

"Sal?" The owner was here. That almost never happened. And who was he talking to? Some guy in a Serpents jacket, greasy hair and torn jeans making him look like an extra from Central Casting for some *West Side Story* summer stock performance.

"Hey, Jughead," Sal called. He waved from across the lot. "Just came in for a meeting." Like this was a law firm or bank and not a drive-in. Like that *Outsiders* greaser was carrying a briefcase and not (most likely) a switchblade in his pocket.

"Just let us know if you hear anything from Lodge," the Serpent was saying in a contrived stage whisper that suggested that he knew I wasn't really supposed to hear the conversation, but also really didn't care.

"I can . . . I can keep you informed." Sal looked uncomfortable, which wasn't how I was used to seeing him. The Twilight was basically his second home—his happy place way more than mine, even.

They shook hands—stiffly—and Sal came over to me. "I see you're on top of things here, Jughead." He was speaking stiffly, too, all mechanical and awkward. "Not that I'd expect anything less."

"Sure. I mean, it's my job." What else did I have to do today, anyway? Interview Dilton Doiley for more details on his doomsday theories? That was a little too *The Number 23* for my taste, thanks.

(Though I had made a note to be sure to press Pop for more dirt on the sordid patronage of the Chock'Lit Shoppe.)

"I'm just going to cash out the register for Ben, get it set for him for tonight," he said. He hooked his thumbs in the front pockets of his jeans. He smelled like drugstore aftershave and sweat. Like he was nervous. Whatever the Serpents were here for, he wasn't happy about it.

"Sounds good," I said. I forced some pep into my voice, Riverdale-style, trying to pretend it was totally normal that he was here, that this wouldn't be the first time we'd be side by side for setup since the week after I was hired. He seemed grateful for my efforts.

I grabbed the trash bag I'd been filling and fished a new pair of gloves out of my pocket, eager to get back to the trash. But before I could, the Serpent was in my face. *He* smelled like sweat, too—but somehow in a menacing way. Sweat and leather and something else I couldn't quite put my finger on—and didn't want to. "Jughead Jones," he said tauntingly. "Look at you, such a choirboy. Doing honest work, collecting *garbage*." He spat the word out like a personal insult.

"Sorry to offend you." I shrugged. I'm not scared of the Serpents, even though plenty of people from Riverdale are.

Yes, they're a gang, and yes, they absolutely are petty thieves and sometime drug dealers. But for the most part, they do their thing and let the good citizens of Riverdale do their own.

A little bit of history: The Serpents date as far back as the 1940s, during the founding of Riverdale. The snake itself and all the laws of the gang were based on Uktena tradition.

The Uktena is a snake, or a water serpent. It's also the name of the indigenous tribe that laid claim to this land before the founders conquered and slaughtered them. Fun fact: The raid was led by General Pickens, whose statue stands proudly in Riverdale's own Pickens Park to this day.

(In that context, it's pretty messed up that the *Serpents* are the ones painted as the enemy in this Manifest Destiny scenario.)

After the raid, the remaining Uktena formed the Serpents as a way of preserving unity among the few of them that were left.

Another fun fact: There was a time when my dad was the Serpents' leader.

Less fun: That directly led to him being demoted at Andrews Construction. (It had been a partnership, but now dad just works there, so that was a thing that Archie and I tried not to talk about.) Which led to him drinking more. Which led to Mom leaving.

Just after she left, he came to me and told me that he was now just a Serpent in name only, that he was breaking off from them in the hopes of cleaning up his act and getting our family back together.

It wasn't going especially well.

It also explained why this guy was so hostile. But that didn't mean I was going to take it without giving a little back, too.

"Does your dad know this is how you earn a living? Does he care that you're basically a janitor?"

Yeah, we talk about it every night, just before he reads me a bedtime story and tucks me in. I mean, he knew I worked at the

Twilight. But we weren't having so many warm and fuzzy conversations these days. For that to be true, he'd have to be home.

"It's too bad, you know, you're out here, sweeping up after the snots in Riverdale. You know your dad could hook you up with some real paying work." He leered. "Want me to get him a message?"

I threw down the trash bag and stepped forward. "What the hell are you talking about?" I said. I'd had enough. "Look, I don't know what to tell you. I'm sorry that my dad defected and you can't get over it or something. But I'm not interested."

He leaned back and laughed, loud and full, like it was the best joke he'd ever heard. "Is *that* what he told you, Junior?" He snorted. "You're so gullible. Sorry to be the one to burst your bubble."

"What?" My stomach sank, but I tried to keep my expression steady. I wouldn't give this guy the satisfaction. Even if what he was saying, confirmation of my worst, steadily growing fears, was sending chills down my spine.

"You think your dad defected? That he's on the straight and narrow now? Why? *Because he said so?* Your mom's gone, right? What does he have left, except the Serpents? Of *course* he'd come back to the fold."

He has ME. His son. Was it that he didn't see that?

Or that he saw it—but it wasn't enough?

"Think about it, Jones. Where do you think he's been spending his days? His nights? He's not sleeping at home, right?"

I looked away, silent.

"He's at the Whyte Wyrm, dumbass." He smirked. "He actually *is* sleeping at home. You were just wrong about where that really is for your pop."

Home. The word had me reeling, disbelief and sorrow swirling through me.

He shoved me, hard enough that I staggered back. I scrambled to come up with something, anything to say, but by the time I got my bearings again, he was already gone.

The Whyte Wyrm. It was a bar on the Southside. I'd seen it, of course. Been inside, too—it wasn't something we Joneses bragged about, but, yeah, I knew enough about Dad's history with the Serpents. Knew that those times, back when I was little, I'd be stuck in the backseat of our beater in the Whyte Wyrm parking lot, nothing to do but make up stories in my head; it was because Dad was in there doing something that, even young, I understood he shouldn't be doing. Something he was slightly ashamed of, but did anyway.

(Remembering that, I realized maybe I have the Serpents to thank for my writing habit, storytelling. Huh. I'd have to be sure to send them a note. When Hell freezes over.)

When I got a little older—middle school, early on—I guess Dad decided I was old enough to take a little more truth. That's when he told me what his jacket really stood for. By then, I already had more than a clue. If Archie Andrews was too white-bread, either too innocent or too kind to spread rumors or pass hearsay along to me, then the Reggie Mantles of the world sure weren't. Dad was a Serpent leader, and I was, incredibly, one of the last to know.

Was I the last again now? Had Dad *really* gone back to it? He promised me.

Then again, it would hardly be the first promise he broke.

"Where do you think he spends his days? His nights?"

Was he not working the construction site, then? I mean, Archie and I were old enough now that we were aware of our fathers' conflicted history. But even if Dad and Mr. Andrews weren't partners anymore, my father still had a job . . . didn't he?

I wanted it to be true. I so badly wanted it to be true. But then, there was *every single thing I already knew about my father* staring me in the face like exhibits A, B, C—hell, the whole freaking alphabet.

I kicked at the trash bag by my feet, anger rising higher as garbage I'd just picked up spewed all over. Stupid. And who was going to have to clean it up again, anyway? Me.

But not right now. Right now, I had something else to do.

I needed to pay a visit to Andrews Construction, immediately.

ARE YOU READY TO
RIDE OR DIE?

SOUTHSIDE
SERPENTS

SERPENT LAWS

1. A SERPENT NEVER SHOWS COWARDICE.

2. NO SERPENT STANDS ALONE.

3. IF A SERPENT'S KILLED OR IMPRISONED, THEIR FAMILY WILL BE TAKEN CARE OF.

~~4. A SERPENT NEVER SHEDS ITS SKIN~~ [REDACTED]

5. NO SERPENT IS LEFT FOR DEAD.

6. A SERPENT NEVER BETRAYS THEIR OWN.

7. IN UNITY, THERE IS STRENGTH.

THE SOUTHSIDE SERPENTS ARE MORE THAN A CLUB. WE'RE A FAMILY. AND WE PROTECT OUR OWN. THINK YOU HAVE WHAT IT TAKES TO JOIN US? YOU'LL HAVE TO GUARD THE BEAST, GRAB THE KNIFE, HANDLE A SNAKEBITE, AND SURVIVE THE GAUNTLET.

IF YOU THINK YOU'RE TOUGH ENOUGH, COME BY THE WHYTE WYRM AND ASK FOR TALL BOY.

Cam:

Where you at, Nicky?

Nick:

Just leaving Ronnie's place. Meeting Tommy
for brunch in 10.

Cam:

OMG and??? Don't leave me hanging.

Nick:

She seemed surprised, but pretty sure she fell for it.

Cam:

Ronnie. Veronica Lodge. Fell for YOU. Doing
what . . . pledging eternal love?

Nick:

Something like that. And YES. B/c as I say,
my charms are irresistible.

Cam:

Try that line on someone who HASN'T been fully
capable of resisting your charms.

Nick:

Never say never, babe.

Cam:

Ew. How about, never say babe.

Nick:

Noted. So where are YOU headed?

Cam:

Meeting Annie at Lalo. We wanted someplace where we wouldn't run into anyone.

Nick:

I feel like u mean, any LODGE.

Cam:

Do you think we're being TOO mean? Messing with V's head when we KNOW what's about to go down? Like, her family's gonna be torn apart & thrown to the wolves & here we're not only cozying up for the live show, but we're screwing with her, too?

Nick:

TOO mean. To Veronica?

Cam:

Well . . .

Nick:

Do you think for a second she'd hesitate to rub it in, if this were happening to any of us? Screw guilt. I'm ready for the show. Might even bring popcorn tonight.

Cam:

Cam:

On my way. Order me a latte with almond milk?

Annie:

You know this place only has soy.

Cam:

OK never mind. Soy. Will pretend like it's 2014 again. Cute. Just texting w/ Nicky. Says Veronica has no idea.

Annie:

HOW? How can she have no idea? Not about us, I mean. But rumors about her dad are EVERYWHERE.

Cam:

Denial, dearie. Denial. I'm sure Marie Antoinette never imagined she'd be captured by the insurgents.

Annie:

Vive la révolution.

CHAPTER ELEVEN

VERONICA

I was still reeling from Nick St. Clair's unexpected visit when I returned to my mom in the dining room, her perfectly painted fingers scrolling purposefully on an iPad. She looked up at me as I came in. "*M'hija*, you look flushed. More than you did when you came up from the gym, that is." She gave me a glance that was one part curiosity, two parts mischief. "What on earth did that boy want?"

I waved my hand. "Oh, what do all boys want, really?" Because the truth is: Though I enjoy male companionship—and I especially enjoy how much all the most sought-after males seek *moi*, of course—I've yet to find that one who truly makes me swoon. And I'm fine with that, for now. It's 100 percent okay if my prospective suitors are the ones doing the majority of the swooning.

"I don't know, Ronnie," Mom said, grinning. "Your words say one thing, but your hot pink cheeks say something else completely."

"We'll see." I rolled my eyes. "He's coming tonight. For which, if I may offer a near-seamless segue, I am now fully available to help with arrangements."

"Take a shower first, *m'hija*. Maybe a cold one."

"Stop."

"Okay, okay. I'll stop. But do take a shower—water temperature of your choice—and then, can you order some cappuccinos and pastries from Lalo? You know which ones I like. I'm having a craving. All this party prep requires some fortification."

"Absolutely," I said, my stomach grumbling at the thought of their Saint Honore tarts gleaming through the glass of their dessert case. "Or I can run out and get them myself, if that's not too long a wait for you. Honestly, it's a gorgeous day, and it's not too punishingly hot out there yet. I wouldn't mind some fresh air." Lalo was about ten blocks uptown, farther than I'd usually venture just for a java fix, but now that Mom had mentioned it, I was having serious cravings, too. And I wanted to walk off some of those spin cramps.

"Not too long a wait at all. Enjoy! On your way out, can you remind Andre that the dresses for tonight should be coming in from the tailor within the hour?"

"Absolutely."

We wore white on the Fourth, of course, and we wore it impeccably fitted. Mine was crochet-lace Chloé, Mom would be in flawless Armani silk pleats.

The Fourth of July was white dresses . . . and red lips. Light and airy, a summer evening dream . . .

But not without a pop of pure, hot fire.

That was signature Lodge, after all.

∧∧∧

When you live as we do, in a Dakota building penthouse duplex, one of the perks is a dedicated elevator down to the lobby level. Announced guests ride up directly into our apartment to be greeted by Smithers. (Another perk? Not having to answer one's own front door.)

As anyone who knows anything about NYC real estate knows, the building itself—an architectural icon—is structured around an ornate shared courtyard, and only accessible through the front gates. A building of its size—with residents of their stature—requires an elaborate staff to function. Though there is, of course, a hierarchy among the staff, each quadrant of the building has its own doorman to oversee it. It's extremely intimate and exclusive. Which is, of course, the entire point.

All of which is an elaborate way to point out that, while I had my elevator ride downstairs all to myself, the lobby was a different story: bustling with the low-key purpose of the privileged class. Even divided into four intimate clusters, it still got a bit congested down here during peak business hours. There was Ms. Leder in coordinated neon athleisure, signing for a Bloomingdale's delivery. There was Hank Golby, wunderkind hedge fund manager, off to spend his requisite two hours in an actual office, Gucci loafers polished even as he no doubt yearned for the comfort of his Rick Owens leather high-tops. There, Tabitha Martindale, blue-haired biddy of the Norma Desmond variety: a former grande dame of the silver screen who now mostly sat around counting her "dolls" (that's prescription pills, to those of you unfamiliar with your Jackie Susann references) and walking her ever-present Papillon, Mama Rose. Today Mama Rose was wearing a tulle skirt in addition to her rhinestone-studded collar; maybe they were coming back from the groomer.

So it wasn't until the lobby that I had any sort of interaction with my neighbors, and by the same token, it wasn't until I interacted with them that I started to wonder if something might be . . . going on? Superficially, it seemed like any other morning. But on a semiconscious level . . .

Call it paranoia, but Daddy says a Lodge can smell subtext. We know when trouble is brewing; it's how we always manage to rise above said trouble. In any case, I waved to Tabitha, like I always do. (I admire her steadfast commitment to keeping Mama Rose on trend.)

And . . . was it my imagination, or did she . . . look away?

I shook my head. Obviously I was seeing things. Projecting for no reason. Very unlike me.

Wait a minute . . . *did Nick St. Clair throw me off my game?*

I debated it. Not possible. Never in a million years. I had low blood sugar from working out and needed more coffee.

Except, as I made my way to the doorman's desk, I saw the shopaholic hausfrau wrinkle her nose slightly as she stepped aside to let me get closer.

Now, *that* wasn't my imagination. Veronica Lodge knows side-eye.

Veronica Lodge basically *invented* it.

I tapped her on the shoulder, a little ashamed of myself that I was even trying to figure this out. *You're better than this, Ronnie.*

Except . . . she shrugged away from me, contracting her shoulder blade like she couldn't bear the physical contact.

I mean, she must have known about our party. *Everyone* knew about our party. It was covered in *Page Six* every year.

So maybe this was nothing more than sour grapes? She was grumpy about not getting an invite? I wouldn't blame her.

I decided it wasn't worth another thought and turned to Andre. I gave him my brightest smile, despite my lingering, underlying unease. "Hello."

"Ms. Veronica," he said. His own mouth was less of a

smile and more of a tight line. This from the same man who gave me drugstore peppermint star hard candies from a glass bowl when I was little.

"Mom just wanted me to let you know that our dresses should be arriving within the hour."

"Of course," he said, looking vaguely pained.

"Are you okay?" I asked, pointed. I was hoping he'd take the out, come clean with some outside concern, some reason— any reason, other than some odd and recently cultivated vendetta—that people, including himself—were suddenly being a little distant.

He cleared his throat, seemed to come back to the moment more confidently. "Of course, Ms. Veronica. Thank you for asking. Actually—" He leaned down, began rummaging in the drawers of his desk. Peppermint candies again, after so many years?

But it was more surprising than that. "Actually, there have been a few messages for you."

I frowned. "Messages? Down here?" Who would call the main desk at the Dakota to try to reach me?

"It's a . . . Lettie Cooper? A young girl, from the sound of it. She said she was calling from a *blog*. The Giggle Girls?"

Uh, never heard of it. Obviously it wouldn't be the first time some wannabe online trend rag hunted me down for a sound bite about the latest in Chanel quilted crossbodies, or where to eat after hours now that Freemans is so overrun by normals. Thanks, but no thanks, I'm not your girl. I don't need the publicity.

No wonder whoever it was couldn't get a direct line to me.

"Thanks," I said. "Did you let Smithers know?" Even if it was just some second-rate tabloid chasing me that he was deliberately stonewalling, he should have passed along the message. That was just part of his job.

He nodded shortly. "I think Mr. Smithers must be excessively busy just now," he said.

"Because of the party?" I mean, I guessed he was right. But we do this party every year. Even though it's a lot of legwork, we have the logistics down. The Lodge women are a well-oiled machine. And Smithers is old-school. Nothing flusters him. It's why he's basically part of the family by now.

"Have a good day, Ms. Veronica," Andre said.

It felt not unlike a dismissal. That was weird, too, for an employee of a building as reputable as the Dakota.

This, too, was starting to feel like something I'd spent too much time on. Obviously there was something in the air today, and I clearly wasn't caffeinated enough.

Whatever, then. To Lalo it was. I know, I know, to most of America, Café Lalo is, first and foremost, that touristy place in that old Meg Ryan movie. Before she made all those regrettable decisions regarding injectables, when she was still America's Sweetheart. I should be above it, I should *only* get my coffee delivered, and then, only from some place with real credentials: Happy Bones in Little Italy or Brooklyn Diamond.

(What? We have a driver; what are they for, if not a spontaneous coffee run into the outer boroughs now and then?)

But Mom has a sweet tooth for Lalo's desserts, and it's been our family's little guilty pleasure for as long as I can remember. And even on summer evenings, when the line wraps around the corner, Daddy ushers us right past the crowd and inside.

Anyway, I don't follow trends, I set them. Lalo may not be edgy or hip, but it's home, and it's mine.

Or at least, I thought it was.

You can imagine my shock when I walked in on the morning of July 3 to find Cam and Annie together, hunched over a honey-glazed brioche, tapping on their cell phones and giggling away. Katie was my bestie, but these girls were full-on extended squad, ever since they befriended Katie and me in sixth grade with tickets to an SNL taping and aftershow invite. (Annie's dad is a producer.) If it was strange that they were having coffee at Lalo, it was even stranger they hadn't invited me along.

Maybe they assumed party prep was keeping me busy. What else could it be? I placed my order (not that I had to; everyone there knows the Lodges; the barista had already starting steaming the milk for my latte when she saw me come in) and swept up to their table.

"Girls! What a pleasant surprise! I thought I was the only Spence student ironic enough to slum it in this *Time Out New York* trap." I leaned down to give them both kisses hello, Euro-style on both cheeks, tilting so they could do the same.

"L-O-L, Ronnie," Cam said, brown eyes sparkling. She took a sip of her drink and gave a satisfied little sigh. "Call us your acolytes."

"I like the sound of that." I raised an eyebrow. "Slide over," I said to Annie, shooing her farther in toward the wall. "I can sit—for a minute."

Annie smiled and shifted. "Great."

"So," I said, elbows on the table. "Everyone ready for tonight?"

The girls exchanged a quick glance that I couldn't quite decipher and then nodded. "*So* ready," Cam agreed, while Annie murmured assent.

"I have a great idea!" I said as the thought hit me. I'm sure I would have thought of it before, if I'd been in town rather than out at the beach. "I have a glam squad coming at four. Why don't you guys join? A little primping pre-party! It'll be so much fun. I'll have the caterers make us a pitcher of white peach sangria. Bobby Flay gave my mom his signature recipe at some benefit in Sag Harbor last week."

"I had—" Annie started.

"Stop," I said. "If you're going to tell me you already have hair and makeup appointments, just cancel them! Who cares? I can adjust my reservation. Come on . . . getting pretty by yourself is boring. It'll be my treat."

"I mean, are you sure?" Cam asked.

What a ridiculous question. "Of course I'm sure! You think Daddy would notice the minor change to the credit card charge? He doesn't even look at my statements. You're coming, and that's final."

Annie let out a strangled little cough, pounding on her chest to catch her breath. "Sorry, I thought that coffee was cooler by now."

"Careful, girl," I said. "You want to be in top shape for the party of the year. I think there might even be some drama to be had tonight."

Cam laughed. "Oh yeah?" Her cheeks were tinged pink, rosier than usual.

"I mean, I probably shouldn't say anything—I don't want to embarrass him, but—I guess it's okay, I trust you guys."

"Duh, obviously you can trust us!" Cam said, redder than ever. Was *her* drink overheated, too? "Ronnie, what are you getting at? Spill now."

I shrugged, trying to show how much of a not-a-big-deal the whole thing was. "Whatever. It's just that . . . Nick came by this morning. It was totally out of the blue."

"Nick came by your house? For no reason?" Cam asked.

"Before noon?" Annie put in.

"I know, I had the exact same thought. But yep, showed up just after I finished working out. Of course, I assumed it was just an elaborate scheme to get a glimpse of me in Lycra, but he actually wanted to talk. He . . . well, he asked me out. Like, on a *date*." Now that I was saying it out loud, it was less adorable and random, and ever-so-slightly more loaded.

Ever-so-slightly more something I might, actually, care a little bit about.

"That's crazy, right?" I asked, more to reassure myself than anything.

There! Another look, again, between Cam and Annie, Cam flushing, and Annie fidgeting with her wiry red curls. But again, maybe it was just me. I mean, I'd just acknowledged that Nick's true confessions had left me a little unsettled. Even if I was only admitting it to myself, for now. I wasn't at my peak form right now, that much was clear.

The silence felt like it dragged on for a beat too long, and I had the weirdest urge to take it all back, shrug and laugh about it, and leave in a rush before anyone could think too much about any of it.

But then, before I could do anything else, Cam burst out laughing.

"*Obviously* that's not crazy, Ron!" she insisted. "I mean, *everyone* knows Nick St. Clair only plays around because he's, like, madly in love with you."

"It's true," Annie jumped in, her hazel eyes suddenly sharp and intense. "Didn't he *tell* you he loved you? Once?"

I made a face, disbelieving. "Uh, that was back when we were in pre-K," I reminded her. "Hardly binding testimony. Back then, my favorite pop star was Barney, remember?"

"Still," she insisted. "Those are formative years. I don't know, maybe you . . . *imprinted* on him or something."

"Like in those vampire books?" Had my girlfriends been body-snatched? Or were they just trying to be supportive, albeit in this vaguely misguided manner?

Cam shot Annie a look like *she* was insane now, then turned back to me. "I think it's just that you guys totally make sense together. Your families go way back. He might be the only guy who could ever handle your father."

She made a good point. "True."

"*And* you have total chemistry."

"Also true." There was no denying the little charge I felt when I looked in his baby blues, even if until now I'd chosen to disregard it. "So you're saying I should go for it?"

All these years, my friends and I had lamented the lack of truly sophisticated, viable options in our circle, bemoaning how we wanted *men* when we were, alas, surrounded by mere boys. High school boys were for practice, if anything. *We can do better* was our mantra, always.

Annie opened her mouth, but Cam elbowed her before she could say anything.

143

"I think what we're saying," Cam said, glancing at Annie, "is that you should just stay open-minded. Hear him out."

"Exactly," Annie said.

My phone buzzed in my bag. I rummaged around and dug it up.

"Oh, ugh. Grace wants me to pick up some accessories from Barneys for a shoot. Great timing." An intern's work is never done.

"Can't they get, like, an assistant to do that?" Annie said.

"I *am* the assistant." I sighed. "It sucks, but it comes with the territory of working with Her Majesty herself, Grace Coddington. I'm her beck-and-call girl." I'd have to grab an Uber if I wanted to get Mom's coffee to her while it was hot and still make it to Barneys in time to get Grace what she needed.

I signaled, and our waitress brought my order to me, steam curling from the lids of the paper coffee cups and the pastries bundled in a white box tied with string. "Don't worry, ladies, we're still on for four. By party time we will have achieved maximum glamour. And as for the . . . other stuff. What can I say, girls? That's certainly some food for thought. It's possible you're on to something."

"You'll think about it?" Cam asked. She looked dubious but oddly hopeful. Oddly invested.

"I will. But for now, we should probably keep this between

the three of us. Nicky would probably be embarrassed to know that I mentioned it to you."

Annie made a lock-and-key motion with her fingers. "Our little secret."

"Perfect." We kissed good-bye and I continued to mull as I wandered back toward the Dakota. *"Stay open-minded."* It sounded like good advice.

Tonight was our party. The holiday was here. Anything could happen.

Cam:

Nicky, you should have seen us, being so normal. In opposite land. HOW is it that she doesn't suspect anything?

Nick:

You know Ronnie: Queen Bee. As in, believes her own hype. She doesn't suspect anything because it would never occur to her to suspect.

Annie:

Karma's a B. And so is Veronica. I cannot WAIT for the party.

Cam:

Speaking of karma, you realize we're probably going to hell, right?

Nick:

Probably? Definitely. And you know what? Worth it.

Annie:

SO worth it.

DILTON DOILEY'S FIELD NOTES:

A blood moon.

Tonight my Scouts will hike to our campgrounds under the light of a blood moon, a full lunar eclipse that paints the sky in muddy red streaks. And while the event has no astrological importance, to me it's undeniably a harbinger. The people of Riverdale want to believe that no bad could ever happen here, despite the insistence that history has of proving us wrong. Evil doesn't cease to exist merely because we refuse to see it. I learned that at too young an age.

My father said he was doing me a favor.

Before the favor, before things changed—before we learned how the world truly is—Dad was an Adventure Scout himself, growing up. He was our troop leader when I was young.

About eight years ago, we had our annual weekend camping trip. But he had an important business trip that week, so he couldn't go. He left my uncle in charge of me for the weekend, and we all went out to Buffalo Flats as planned.

We spent the first day working on our adventure badges, doing arts and crafts, archery—simple stuff. The next day was the real event of the weekend—the annual whitewater rafting excursion. My uncle came with me in my raft.

It had been a long, snowy winter, and the river was full and fast. It was all we could do to stay upright. It was exhilarating, a huge rush—until…

We went over a giant rapid, one our guide didn't know was there. In a moment, most of us were underwater. My head was spinning from whiplash. I yelled for my uncle, but couldn't see him. It was all I could do to get to shore.

We couldn't pull together a rescue attempt. We didn't even have a rope—nobody had thought to bring one. Some Scouts we were.

My dad was…well, he's not very emotional. But I could tell he was upset. He had lost his only brother. He was not going to lose me…No matter what it took.

"Son," he said. "You will never be unprepared again."

He meant it—never. Not for any of the inevitable horror that awaits us all.

And so, he trained me. A series of tests began. Hours, days, weeks spent alone together, Dad showing me all types of survivalist skills: knot tying, knife throwing, how to identify poisonous flora, how to purify any water source. How to spot a predator from any and every approach.

He even had me defusing IEDs—unsuccessfully.

"If that had been a real bomb, we'd both be dead," he told me that time.

"I'm sorry. I can't—" I was just a kid. I was terrified, ashamed. I didn't know what was real and what wasn't.

The "trials" kept escalating, until one day, we were leaving the grocery store. He handed me a necktie. "Put this over your eyes, son."

We drove a long time. An hour, maybe two. I lost track. The asphalt and smoke in the air—smells of Riverdale, of the town—gradually faded away.

He took me out into the woods—so similar to the same Sweetwater Woods my Scouts and I have hiked so often, where we'll make our camp tonight. He brought me to a clearing and sat me down on the rotted-out trunk of a fallen tree. The wood was spongy underneath me.

"I don't have to tell you: The world is tough and unforgiving," he said, words that I'd eventually parrot to Jughead Jones—foolish, cynical Jughead!—"You've seen that yourself, younger than a boy should have to. You've come a long way, Dilton."

Had I? I wasn't so sure. But he was my father, I had to trust him.

"You've come a long way," he said again. "This is your final test.

"I believe in you, son. I believe you can do this." Solemnly, he handed me a Swiss Army Knife, the red enamel shiny and new. It's the Knife I carry at all times, the Knife I was carrying when Weatherbee suspended me this year for having a weapon on school grounds.

Like I cared about a suspension. Like I'd ever leave the house without it, without protection of some Kind.

No, Dad taught me too well. He left me in those woods that day.

When he got back into the car, I thought that he was just trying to scare me, that he'd be back in an hour. But then it got cold. And dark. And I began to realize: I was on my own.

Needless to say, I did it. Nine days out in Fox Forest, all alone. Only my Knife and my own skills to rely on. I lived off berries; I found fresh drinking water. I was, eventually, able to trap and cook a squirrel. It was the only time in my life I've had to hunt another living creature. It was difficult, but it was what I had to do. Eventually, I found my way back to town.

It was hard—excruciating, really, not to mention terrifying at times—but I'm not bitter. I understand. My dad did it so I could learn to live off the land. So I could learn how to make it through hardship. Because *life* is a hardship. A series of tests.

And since then, I've dedicated myself to preserving my father's code of survival over someone like Principal Weatherbee's, with his ridiculous rules and regulations and complete unwillingness to see beneath the veil. For better or for worse, for all of us.

The apocalypse is nigh. If I sound like a raving lunatic, so be it. I plan to be prepared and to keep my Scouts safe. In order to keep them safe, they must be with me.

Jones didn't believe me, of course. That's typical. But I know. I may just be the only one in Riverdale who does know.

How can I be so sure? It's simple.

Because of Baley's Comet. It graces the sky once every eight years.

Or, at least, it used to.

Twenty years ago, the cycle began to speed up. Now the comet shows up every nine months. It's getting closer to us.

Tonight we will see our fourth blood moon in as many months, an event long prophesized to signal the end times.

When the moon rises red in the sky, after we've made camp, I will present my argument to the Scouts:

Our fourth blood moon in four months. The comet growing closer with each cycle.

The path unfolding is inevitable, inarguable. Soon enough, Baley's Comet will slam into North America, causing an extinction event not seen since the dinosaurs.

I'm talking about the end of the world.

I know—it sounds dramatic.

But I promise you, it doesn't sound remotely dramatic enough.

I will make them see, these boys. Make them understand what fate awaits us.

And then, once we're home again, I'll show them. What I've been working on for so long, now. My pet project, our salvation. My father's *real* final test.

I have a space. I built it myself, outfitted it perfectly. It's small, but it's safe. Private. I've got the basics covered, plans drawn out to provision it. We'll need to equip ourselves:

Water.

Defense.

Better defense.

Endurance.

Strength.

It's a survival bunker, of course. It took my dad and me five years to build it. It has an independent generator that runs off a mix of solar and natural gas, so it's completely off the grid. I've got enough water and canned food to last for months. Years, if we ration. The walls are lined with an inch of pure lead to keep out all forms of radiation.

It's everything we need to wait out the apocalypse.

The boys may balk, at first. They may be reluctant to believe that their idyllic Riverdale could ever be a danger, could ever be a threat to them, to their existence.

But they'll see the blood moon. They'll hear my stories.

Eventually, they'll come around.

CHAPTER TWELVE

ARCHIE

It was almost high noon at the construction site when I saw Dilton Doiley and his troop ride by on their bikes, their bright orange Adventure Scout flags waving from their backseats in the wind. Their bikes were loaded down with gear, everyone hunched over their handlebars, throwing their whole bodies into it to hustle forward.

I had to hand it to Dilton. He was wound a little tight—okay, more than a little—but whatever it was specifically that made him tick, he'd found his tribe in those Scouts, a group that would never question him, whose loyalty was completely steady.

In theory, I had that, too, with the Bulldogs. Thinking of them gave me a twinge in my gut. I was dreading the message from Reggie I knew was coming about a prank retaliation. Or, I was dreading having to tell him I couldn't do it. Never mind that I didn't even really *want* to.

If my loyalties were so divided, what kind of teammate was I, now? What kind of person?

"Hey, Red—you want to share that wire rope, or were you planning on asking it to the prom?"

"What? Oh, sorry." I looked up to find Lenny, my dad's foreman for this job, standing over me, eyeing my wheelbarrow and laughing. "Just bringing it over to that pile." I pointed. "I, uh, got distracted."

"I'll say. You've been standing here for almost ten minutes straight, staring into space. Your dad sent me out here to tell you to meet him in the trailer."

"What? No, I can finish loading the wire—"

"I got it," he told me, winking and moving to grab the wheelbarrow handles. "Don't you know, kid? When the boss whistles, you come running."

"Right," I said. Even when the boss was your dad. Or maybe make that *especially* when the boss was your dad.

I ran. I guess it turns out, I do still have some sense of loyalty inside.

Dad was at his desk, hunched over a set of blueprints, his hard hat next to him and a pencil in his hand. He looked totally caught up in the plans, lost in concentration, but when the door banged shut behind me, he looked up and smiled. "Archie. How is it out there?"

"Everything's moving," I said, wiping my forehead with the back of my arm. It didn't help much, only managed to mix some dust from my arm in with the sweat on my face. Turns out, that's what construction comes down to, in a nutshell: dust and sweat, and eventually, something new gets built up out of all the effort.

When Dad first approached me about working for him at the beginning of the summer, I didn't realize how satisfying it would be, actually making something, creating something physical that you could touch and see, from your own two hands. It wasn't music, that was for sure. But it was still way more creative than I expected, to be honest.

"Lenny said you wanted to see me?"

"Yep." He nodded at the chair across from his desk and reached for a brown paper bag on a nearby shelf. "Thought you might want some lunch. That stuff you brought from Pop's this morning is long gone, sorry to say, but we've got tuna and rye from that Greendale deli, if you're hungry. And iced tea. It's a hot one out there."

"Yeah, you don't have to tell me that," I agreed, grabbing the tea and gulping it down in almost one go. My appetite was insane since I started construction. Bigger even than during training season. "But, ah . . . what's the rest of the crew going to think? You always calling me in here, letting me sit and eat in the air-conditioning while other guys are slaving away in the blazing sun? It's pretty blatant nepotism."

Dad's forehead wrinkled up. "What will they *think*? They'll think I'm a good father." He laughed. "They already think I'm a good boss. I'm not worried about their opinion of me. My men and I are good."

"Fair enough." If he wasn't worried, neither was I. I settled in and unwrapped a sandwich.

(Speaking of loyalties, Pop would not be happy to see this. But he gets more than enough of our business. This was barely a drop in the bucket.)

Thinking of Pop's made me think of Jughead, which brought me back to our conversation last week. It was cool that he was writing; funny that both of us were doing some of that these days, even if mine were songs and his were stories. It just went to show that even now, when we didn't spend nearly as much time as we used to together, Jug and I were always, in some way, on each other's wavelength. I guess that's what old friends are like.

Oh, no. In a flash, I remembered two things: First, that Jug and I were supposed to go to Centerville tomorrow, and I wouldn't be able to. Second, that the reason I wouldn't be able to was because of my plans with Geraldine. Plans I still hadn't told my dad about.

Speaking of loyalty . . . I hated to lie to my dad. So far, things with Geraldine had mostly been lies of omission; I just hadn't told him what I'd been up to recently. Either he flat-out couldn't tell that I was being cagey, or he didn't want to admit it to either of us, to put it out there in way that meant we'd *have* to deal with it, whether we wanted to or not.

But like it or not, I was going to be away overnight tonight. Dad wasn't super nosy or in my face, but I needed to account for that. Especially with Mom being gone, Dad was more attentive than ever, trying to make sure I still felt like we had stability at home and stuff. Trying to make sure I knew my parents still loved me, and that he, in particular, was still 100 percent there for me.

It made it even harder to be dishonest, white lie or no.

It was like he could read my mind—spooky, but another check in the "Dad's there for you" column. He put down his own sandwich and took a quick sip of water. "I don't think you told me for sure—do you have plans for the holiday? You must."

My throat went all hot. I had practiced this in my mind a thousand times: what I was going to tell him, how I was going to say it. The best lies (*white lies*, I insisted to myself) all start with an element of truth, right?

"Uh, Jug and I, we were going to hang out," I started.

What could be more believable? Jughead and I spent the Fourth together every year. We even talked about meeting up this year, too.

"*Independence Day* at the Twilight, huh?"

"Yeah. And I was gonna stay at his place. Tomorrow we'll go down to Centerville like usual. Well, not totally usual.

Betty won't be there." A fist clenched and unclenched in my stomach while I spoke, misleading Dad, and using Jug for an alibi. Then bringing up Betty for a hat trick. Whatever thread I was holding on to for my loyalty card, it was unraveling pretty fast.

"Right, right. Betty. How's her internship going?"

There was that twinge again, this time right under my ribs. The thing was, I didn't know that much about how Betty's internship was going. We'd barely talked or texted since she left.

It wasn't anyone's fault. But she was out doing . . . well, doing her LA thing. And I was here, with music . . . and Geraldine.

It wasn't anyone's fault, but things change.

But I couldn't say any of that to Dad. "Um, it's good. She's good. She's having fun." Knowing Betty, that had to be true. She was great at everything she did, all the time. Why would this be any different?

It's just a lie of omission, I told myself. *A white lie. Barely even untrue.*

"Glad to hear it," Dad said. "Although I miss having her around. You guys make a cute couple."

I blushed, the curse of being a redhead. "Dad, we're not a couple; you know that."

"Could've fooled me. I mean, I know that's your story and you're sticking to it, but you sure do act like a couple.

Spending all your time together. And she obviously adores you. You could do a lot worse."

"Betty's amazing," I agreed. Because she was. Is. She is literally the platonic ideal of the girl next door: beautiful, kind, devoted, smart. It's not any big mystery why we're so tight. "But, she doesn't, you know, *adore me*. I mean not in that way. We're just friends. It's possible for a guy and a girl to be friends, you know."

"I didn't say it wasn't," Dad agreed. "But I've also seen the way she looks at you. If you want to play dumb, son, that's your call. And maybe you're not looking to take your friendship with her to the next level, that's cool. But you should just be aware. And, you know, be sensitive."

"Jeez, Dad." What was with the "very special episode" talk? I didn't need a reminder from anyone about how to behave with Betty. She wasn't, like, a "girl" that way, that needed to coddled. That's what's so great about her—or one of the things, anyway. Betty's like a guy friend, like a best bud—only better.

Dad put his hands up flat in a "back off" gesture. "All right, all right. Point taken. You and Betty are one hundred percent platonic. The platonic ideal of platonic. Just friends."

"Just friends."

"So . . ." He got a devilish look in his eye. "You're a red-blooded American teenage boy."

"Yeah?" I was wary.

"It's just, if Betty's not the one . . . there's gotta be some-one else, right? I can't imagine you're just sitting up there in your bedroom playing video games all alone, like a monk." He gave me a look. "Don't think I haven't noticed you head-ing out at night after dinner." My mouth opened in surprise, but he didn't let me get a word in. "Don't worry, I'm not gonna get on your case, Arch. You think I wasn't the same way at your age? Sneaking out the back door when my par-ents weren't looking so I could meet up with girls?"

"So you could meet up with Mom?" It was no secret he and Mom had been high school sweethearts, even if these days, those hearts were a little more beat-up, worse for the wear.

"Sure, Mom." He smirked.

"What's that look?" Did I want to know? This whole man-to-man thing with my dad was a little much.

"I was no monk either, Arch. There was your mom, and there were some other girls here and there. What can I say?"

What *couldn't* he say? What *hadn't* he said? This little gos-sip session was getting a little too up close and personal.

"So?" He looked at me, expectant. "Where is my erst-while son going at night, when he disappears out the door? Who's the lucky lady?"

I flashed to Geraldine, sizing me up from behind those heart-shaped sunglasses as I trudged along the side of the road. Geraldine, in the backseat of that same car, later.

161

Geraldine, this morning in her house, sunlight streaming through the windows, lighting her up from behind.

"Come on, Dad," I protested. "It's not like that. No lady. I've just been running. Coach Clayton was real specific about us needing to stay in shape over the summer."

Dad raised an eyebrow. "Running. Sure."

"Running."

"You know pouring concrete is as good a workout as any of the Bulldogs'll have in the off-season."

"I know," I said, grateful to be off the topic of girls. "Speaking of—" I jerked my head in the direction of the trailer door.

"Yeah, yeah, go get back to it—before I'm accused of *blatant nepotism*," Dad said, smiling. "Will I see you before you go to Jug's tonight?"

"Uh, maybe?" Geraldine and I still hadn't finalized our plans for meeting up.

"I'm glad you're staying there," Dad said, almost like an afterthought. "Jughead could probably use a friend right now, what with FP—" He stopped abruptly, as though he just realized he was taking the conversation in a direction he hadn't planned on.

"What with FP, what?" I asked. What was my dad not telling me?

"Never mind. I'm just rambling. You guys have fun. Let me know how Jug's doing."

"Will do," I said, wondering why my dad would be curious about Jughead's state. Wondering what it was *he* wasn't telling *me*.

I guess I wasn't the only one telling little white lies these days.

Not a lie, I corrected myself. *An omission.*

Dad was *omitting* things, hiding things from me.

It didn't really sound that much better.

Ben:

You sure you can't see me today? I miss you!

Geraldine:

Today's not going to work. I have plans.

Ben:

But—

Geraldine:

I said, I have plans. Your lesson isn't until next week. If you come sooner it might look suspicious.

Ben:

Aren't you sick of sneaking around, tho? Wouldn't you rather just have everything out in the open?

Geraldine:

I understand you're frustrated. But once this is out in the open it is all over. Is that really what u want? Wouldn't you rather just be patient instead?

Ben:

I guess. But I don't like it.

Geraldine:

Enjoy the 4th. I'll see you next week.

CHAPTER THIRTEEN

BETTY

By all accounts, Veronica Lodge is an intelligent, confident, raven-haired—and silver-tongued—beauty, mistress of all she surveys as a sophomore sophisticate at the tony NYC Spence Academy. The daughter of Hiram and Hermione Lodge—yes, *those* Lodges, magnates of Lodge Industries— this pampered sub-deb seemingly holds her universe in the palm of her (well-manicured, natch) hand.

What's your vision of the ideal high school it girl? We promise you, Veronica has it all: Brains? Check. Beauty? Check. A bottomless bank account, a #rideordie #girlsquad of similar "haves," and the choice of any male suitor who suits her fancy?

Check. Check. Check.

Rumor has it Veronica "Ronnie" Lodge once bought out the entire shoe section at Saks so no other student could sport the same stilettos she was rocking (I guess girlfriend's never heard of Zappos?).

Few are willing to go on the record saying anything *against* dear old Ronnie, but, then, why should they, when The Lady herself has been known to laughingly self-identify as "a shallow, toxic rich bitch who ruins everything in her path?"

Okay, then. #Sorrynotsorry.

Daddy Dearest has been known to play it fast and loose with the wolves of Wall Street, but so far, rumblings from the underclass aside, no charges have stuck. And while, by all accounts, Veronica excels at basically everything she puts her mind to (seriously: the girl can sing, dance, and quote high literature at the drop of a straight-off-the-runway hat), we're told she has a special aptitude for math: aka a head for business.

Why settle for simply inheriting your parents' business when you could dominate it instead? The future of Lodge Industries may well be female.

Dear Diary:

Two hours and countless Google rabbit holes later, and this was as far as I'd gotten with my story on Veronica Lodge. The girl was inaccessible to the highest degree, so instead of relying on the proverbial horse's mouth, I thought I'd do a little digging of my own.

But there just weren't any bones to be found.

Truly, this Veronica sounded terrible—a benevolent dictator who thought her looks and her wealth entitled her to run roughshod over other people's lives, wants, dreams. But those who didn't want to be her or be *with* her were downright terrified of her. No one outright said it anywhere, but a little bit of poking around on the Spence student forums made it abundantly clear.

(BTW—creating a fake handle for those boards? That was so easy, even Nancy Drew herself would've been bored by the process.)

There were open letters about bullying—one horror story in particular about some poor girl being forced to drink gutter water, which in NYC had to be next-level gross—but none went so far as to name names. It was easy enough to connect the dots when you read months' worth of letters and columns back to back, piecing together the periphery players and trying to find the common thread.

The real dirt was on Hiram Lodge, who was some kind of Wall Street tycoon. Back last spring, he ran some kind of investment deal that a bunch of financial consultants were calling Bernie Madoff levels of shady. But again—no one had gone fully on the record, and so far, nothing had interfered with the Lodges' comfortably padded life of luxury. Her personal Instagram was locked, and her public Instagram was cluttered with heavily curated shots of clothing racks at

Barneys, Bendel's . . . what looked like a private fitting with . . . Christian Siriano . . . for the Met Gala??? Yup, followed by a shot of a custom-designed pair of coordinating #JimmyChoos, which I didn't know real, not-movie-star people actually wore.

She got her hair and makeup done by Paul Podlucky on the Upper East Side, along with Kendall Jenner and the other Estée Lauder models, and she used to work out at Tone House before she decided it was too crowded and had her father build her a personal spin studio in their apartment. She and Taylor Swift were spotted sporting ironic matching manicures in the front row at Nanette Lepore at last year's Fashion Week. She was asked to be a guest judge on *Project Runway: Junior* with Ariana Grande, but she demurred because she had plans to be at Necker (you know, Richard Branson's private island) that week. Where she was—wait for it—"unwittingly" snapped in a candid liplock with the male Hadid.

So what was there to say about the girl that she hadn't already said herself?

Well, I'd never know, anyway. Not the way my afternoon was going.

Rebecca had teased the idea of getting out of the office early, what with the holiday and everything. But the air in the place had changed since "Backpack-gate," and even though she, Cleo, and I were basically sitting at our respective desks watching metaphoric paint dry (or in my case, concocting third-party "interviews" about a pathologically elusive subject), I certainly wasn't going to raise the issue again.

Cleo . . . Glancing over past the bullpen toward the reception desk, I found myself wondering again: *Could* she have been the one who planted that stuff from the closet? We *were,* actually, supposed to be a "respectful environment," like Rebecca had said. But I knew as well as anyone: Girls don't always play that way. Had I made an enemy of Cleo, somehow? Enough so that she'd go out of her way—like even endangering her own reputation at the website—to destroy me?

I couldn't think of anything I might have done to get on Cleo's bad side. But some girls don't need an excuse. Didn't all those stories I dredged up about Veronica Lodge basically say as much? Maybe that was the first hard lesson I'd have to learn as LA Betty.

Well, I know one thing for certain: LA Betty isn't going down that easy.

THINGS I KNOW ABOUT CLEO:
1) She wears cool glasses
2) She has super-shiny hair
3) She's basically never said more than a few
   sentences to me at a time, and those

sentences were usually things like, "There's cake in the break room," or "Rebecca wants those yoga sock samples, like, right now." To which I responded, "Oh! Thanks," and "Sure!" respectively.

Look, everybody doesn't have to love everybody all the time. It's fine. Maybe some people think I'm a goody-goody, or too plain-Jane. I'm for sure not an LA hipster.

We're not all going to be besties. But in the few weeks I've been at *Hello Giggles*, I couldn't think of anything I might have done to get on anyone's bad side, and certainly not Cleo's in particular. Mostly I just do my coffee runs, keep my head down, file what needs to be filed, and pray that maybe, just maybe, I'll eventually be given a real assignment.

And then today, I was.

Hmm.

Not just one assignment, either. The wallpaper *and* the Veronica Lodge profile.

I mean, I knew it wasn't because Rebecca had suddenly seen some great promise in me. I happened to be in the right place—a mostly deserted office—at the right time. Who are we kidding? But, I don't know—if Cleo had writing aspirations of her own, maybe my sudden jump up the editorial ladder was a threat.

It was the best explanation I could come up with.

Was Cleo waiting for a byline of her own? Did she want it so badly that she was willing to *plant evidence in my bag* to frame me?

And if so, what would she do next?

Look, I'm a lover, not a fighter. But whoever went through my stuff threw the first punch. Whatever happens now is just self-defense.

Including, for example, going through Cleo's files to figure out if—and why—she's out to get me.

Her phone was the obvious choice. But she was attached to it like it was a life-sustaining organ. She even took it with her to the bathroom. (Side note: gross.) After about an hour of low-key stalking her movements throughout the office, I learned that the hard way.

I was putting the finishing touches on my Veronica Lodge placeholder piece—clearly, it wouldn't be done until I got a freakin' quote from her highness herself, but something was better than nothing, and this was going to have to do for now—when I finally saw her shiny, shiny hair cascade over her shoulders as she pushed away from the reception desk. She hadn't so much as twitched in her chair in the last sixty minutes, so this felt like a moment to seize. She vanished to the bathroom. I couldn't tell if she'd brought her phone with her.

Rebecca was back in the conference room, poring over layouts or something "manage-y" like that. So she wasn't around to see me being decidedly disrespectful of my coworker and her personal space. *Bonus.* I crept toward the reception desk with my own phone and a thumb drive in my pockets. (Nancy Drew would never embark on an investigation unprepared, and neither would I.)

Papers were scattered everywhere. (For a digital workplace, we generated a ton of printouts. Being analog and retro was kind of on-brand for our team. Honestly, if I came in one day to find Rebecca writing copy longhand with some insane feather pen, it wouldn't shock me one bit.) I grabbed my phone and took pictures of anything and everything—I had no idea what might end up being a clue.

I only had a few moments, but from what I could see it was mostly press release samples, marked-up with red pencil and bright Post-it flags. *Okay, nothing to do with me.* Before today, I wasn't trusted with drafting anything so official as a press release. They didn't even usually circulate to my desk. Her work ID was there, too, the sharp angles of her cheekbones staring ahead at the camera intently.

I shivered. Cleo had never been warm and fuzzy. But with the possibility of being a target in her sights, that severe expression felt way more ominous. I snapped a picture of her ID. I had no idea what I'd use it for—to find out precisely when she'd logged in and out of the building? Who cared?— but it was more information. That was comforting.

"Do you need something, Betty?"

I jumped. *Very stealthy.* I'd been wrapped up in getting pictures of Cleo's desk and hadn't heard her come back from the bathroom. Total amateur hour. Nancy Drew would be ashamed.

Thinking quickly, I shoved my phone—and its creepy, incriminating photos—back in my pocket. "Sorry, I had a question for you about . . . Rebecca's schedule, but I got a text while I was waiting for you."

"Uh-huh." She didn't look convinced. "Well, she'll probably be here until regular end-of-day hours tonight, even with the holiday. She's not one for knocking off early. Sorry to disappoint." She made a face that wasn't all that believable.

"Right. Oh well." I thought about it. Was there *any* way this could work to my advantage? "And you'll be here, too?" Maybe I'd get another crack at her computer.

Was I *willing* to take a crack at her computer? Like, actually go through her files?

I thought I was. LA Betty was.

"If Rebecca's here, I'm here," she said. She set her mouth in a tight line.

I tried to look pleased by this news. "Of course. Um, me too."

"Of course," Cleo said. "Yay."

Sarcasm. That was new.

Well, LA Betty? On to Plan B.

From: WWeatherbee@GoBulldogs.edu
To: [list: All_Bulldog_Football]
Re: Pranks

To all varsity Bulldog football players:

Coach Clayton has informed me of the recent discovery of a prank that took place on our football field. By now you've all no doubt heard that the turf was discovered spiked with plastic forks. Whoever the culprit, it was indeed a very thorough job.

Though Custodian Svenson has offered to clean up, Coach Clayton and I have discussed the matter, and we agree that the Bulldogs should be responsible for cleaning the field together. Regardless of who committed the act, cleaning it together should prove to be an effective team-building exercise.

We realize, of course, that the vandals responsible for the prank may not be Riverdale students. In fact, it is entirely plausible that this is an act of defiance from one of our athletic rivals. Note that the school's official policy on such "prank wars" is zero tolerance; we expect our students to comport themselves like the mature, dignified Riverdale High ambassadors that they are, and to refrain from any retaliation.

Thank you.

From: RMantle@GoBulldogs.edu
To: [list: My_Dawgs]
Re: Pranks

Yo—I know the Bee wants us to lay low, and I guess that's Coach's official position on the prank thing, too. But we're not gonna take this lying down, are we?

Meet after the movie tonight at the Twilight and come with your best ideas for revenge. Don't let me down, dawgs.

Archie:

Sorry, Reg. Won't be able to make it tonight.

Reggie:

Andrews! Where's your team spirit?

Archie:

Can't. Sorry.

Reggie:

Not good enough.
The team needs you.

Archie:

Maybe after 4th. Don't know. Got stuff going on.
I'll think about pranks, if I can. Maybe
something else?

Reggie:

Dude.

Reggie:

OK, man. I just hope u figure out your
loyalties before season starts up again.

CHAPTER FOURTEEN

JUGHEAD

It took forever and it was hot as hell outside, but I walked from the Twilight to Andrews Construction's latest site. I knew where it was, of course, even if I hadn't seen Dad actually leave for work yet, and Archie and I weren't spending much time together. With the place I was in mentally, if I'd been home I would have just said *screw it*, grabbed Dad's bike, to hell with what he'd say. If what that Serpent told me about him was true, he wasn't in any position to be giving me orders.

But fired up as I was, there was a not-so-small part of me that was still—against all rational thought—hoping it wasn't true.

Even if I'd never actually *seen* him to go work. Not once since the summer started. And maybe going back further?

Was I really that self-involved that I couldn't even remember?

My stomach started jumping as the site came into view: the backhoe loader grinding along, chewing up the dry earth, and coughing big clouds of dust and debris. It dawned on me that Archie might be here now. Probably *would* be here. Somehow, I'd missed that. And then what? He was obviously avoiding me. If I randomly showed up at his work, he wasn't going to be thrilled.

Who cares? I decided, amped up as ever. *Why should I be the only one walking around feeling rubbish all the time? Who cares if* he's *uncomfortable when he's the one who's been dodging me! Let him answer, own up to his stuff, just for once.*

Each step I took churned up my righteous indignation, cranked it up another notch. I may be the dark, cynical weirdo of Riverdale High, fine. But this rage—black and hot like my chest was full of tar—was kind of next-level, even for me.

I flashed back to Pop telling Dilton and me about the people who'd come through the diner in his time. *Bonnie and Clyde*—it was insane. And how his father claimed to have had a premonition, or a . . . a *something* about them, at the time. I didn't buy into that kind of New Age woo-woo stuff, but Pop sure seemed to mean what he was saying. And then there was Dilton, doing his full-on Cassandra, doomsday soothsayer. "*A blood moon*," he'd said. And now *my* blood was bubbling inside me, a fury-fueled pact.

No, I didn't buy into what Pop had been going on about. But there, stalking forward toward Mr. Andrew's trailer in the blazing midday sun? That was the first time I felt, in my core, like there might be some truth to the idea that there is—there's always been—an evil lurking at the heart of Riverdale.

That it might be getting ready to rise, to sink its claws into me. Into all of us.

That we might not escape unscathed.

$\sim\!\sim\!\sim$

Mr. Andrews looked genuinely surprised when I burst into his trailer. He actually jumped a little in his seat when the door banged shut. Behind me, I heard Lenny, the foreman, shouting, "Hey! You can't just barge in there. Mr. Andrews is working." But I *could* just barge in there and I *would* just barge in there and I *was,* so whatever, Lenny.

Even startled, Mr. Andrews was much more sanguine than Lenny had been. Whatever he was working on, he folded it neatly and packed it away in a desk drawer. "Jughead," he said, like he was happy to see me. Maybe even expecting me. "You just missed Archie."

"Yeah," I grumbled, hooking a thumb into my back pocket. "Seems like that's been happening a lot lately." But was I missing Archie, or just, you know, *missing* Archie, in the technical sense? It was hard to tell. Probably some combination of the two.

"Really?" Mr. Andrews arched an eyebrow. "And here I always assumed you two were thick as thieves."

I smiled despite myself. "Mr. Andrews," I said, "I don't have any grandparents left. But even if I did, I don't think even they would use the expression 'thick as thieves.'" I knew the mild teasing wouldn't bother him.

Like I expected he would, he just shrugged good-naturedly. "Attached at the hip. Inseparable. *Bosom buddies.*" He winked. "How about that?"

I shook my head. "You're killing me, man."

"Don't you mean, *Old Man*?"

Jeez, why did this guy have to be so damn charming, even when I was worked up? Of course, that was true about Archie, too. It's why he gets away with anything and everything.

"Haven't you heard? A million is the new billion. In terms of age, I mean." I took the liberty of having a seat across from him.

Thinking about Archie, though, and our former inseparability—that was all I needed to bring me back to the original purpose of my meeting. Not to mention, bring me down a bit.

"Anyway, yeah. Arch and I are both, you know . . . busy," I finished lamely. Lamely because, *duh*, it was summer, and how busy could a teenage boy possibly be? Yeah, Archie had his job, and, fine, I had my writing . . . but neither of those things were so completely all-consuming. And neither explained why we suddenly were the polar opposite of *thick as thieves*.

"I know, I know," Fred said, which made me sad for a minute, because of how much he *didn't* know. (Do any of us?) "I worry I'm working him too hard. And then he's out all night. What are you guys up to, anyway? How many milk shakes can two boys drink, even strapping young men like yourselves?" A deep groove appeared between his eyes, the kind that said he really *was* worried about this, even though he was trying to be cool about it.

Out all night. And Mr. Andrews didn't know where. He thought Archie and I were hanging out. At *Pop's*, since we obviously weren't at his house. *Hmm.*

Whatever the situation with Archie, I wasn't going to give him up. I'm no narc. "A lot, Mr. Andrews. But then, you knew that about me. Eating is basically my superpower."

"Always was, Jug. Very true." He shuffled some papers out of the way and leaned his forearms on the desk. "I've gotta tell you, I was relieved when he said you two were going down to Centerville tomorrow like you used to. A little return to normalcy will be good for Archie." He sighed.

"He doesn't talk about it much, but I think his mom leaving was harder on him than I expected."

"Yeah, I guess that's normal." I couldn't say I was taking my own mom's leaving all that well, either.

But then, that wasn't the headline here. The real news was that Archie had told his father about our plan to head to Centerville—even though he'd been blowing me off pretty aggressively ever since we made those plans in the first place. So, either he really *did* plan to see me tomorrow . . . or he was using me as his alibi.

I hated that the second option seemed so much more likely than the first.

I hated, too, that I *still* was no narc. I wouldn't be the one to tell Fred Andrews Archie was otherwise engaged for the Fourth.

"Totally normal. He needs his space," Mr. Andrews said, jolting me back into the moment. "I'm even going to be gracious about the fact that he's sleeping at your place the night before the holiday. What can I say? I'm a martyr."

"Sleeping over?" My voice went up. Archie *never* slept over, not even when things really *were* normal. There was just so much more space at his house.

I coughed and adjusted my tone. "Yeah, well. Good old days, blah, blah. It'll be fun. Like we're ten again. It's just too bad we're too small for the tree house these days."

Mr. Andrews raised his eyebrows. "If you're asking me to

build another one, don't bother. I've got my hands more than full here, if you can't tell."

"I can tell, I can tell." I paused, took a deep breath. This was my moment. I just needed to come out and say it. "Speaking of . . . you've got a full crew out there. Is my dad around? I didn't see him on my way in."

"Your . . . dad?" Mr. Andrews's face went through a series of expressions: confusion, surprise . . . and finally remorse.

My heart sank. There it was. The truth I'd been working so hard to avoid.

"Jug," Mr. Andrews said, softly this time, in a way that made my throat tighten at just the suggestion of his pity. "Your dad's not here."

I was silent, waiting for the proverbial other shoe to drop.

Mr. Andrews suddenly looked extremely uncomfortable. *Good.* That made two of us, anyway. "That's, ah, one of the reasons I was glad Arch would be staying with you tonight. I was . . ." He looked like he was debating how to say what he was thinking, *if* he should say it.

Finally, he leveled me with an even look. "Jug, you know your father and I go way back. He's like a brother to me."

I said nothing, just steadily returned his gaze.

"But, you know, people change, they evolve, they grow apart . . . and, you know, it's sad—god knows it's practically tragic—but there's not always anything to do about it."

My dad and Mr. Andrews were like brothers? Yeah, they were. So were Arch and me, once. And Mr. Andrews was like a second father to me—one who was reliable, a TV dad who packed lunches and walked the dog. I never, ever expected I'd be sitting across from him now, everything—all our families' connections, our friendships, our trust—having completely eroded.

The word hit me like a slap across the cheek. *Alcoholic.* We all knew it, of course. But we didn't call it by its name.

His shoulders slumped. "You must have seen some of it. I don't know, maybe he hid it at home. I know I would have tried to. But at a certain point, it's impossible to hide. Not completely." He reached across the desk to take my hand, but I pulled back. This wasn't some health class promo film, it was my *life.* "Anyway, the details aren't that important. It's the same story that so many know so well. It's a disease, you know."

"*I know,*" I said through gritted teeth. Like I needed *Fred Andrews* making excuses for my father.

Like there *were* any excuses to be made.

"So like I said, that was why I was glad to hear Archie was going to stay with you tonight. I know . . . well, let's just say, Riverdale's a pretty small town. Word gets around. I know your father hasn't been sleeping at home. So I thought you could use the company."

There was a spot on the linoleum floor of the trailer, a black smear like the scuff of a sneaker tread. I focused on that spot like it contained the secrets of the universe.

"Where's my dad, Mr. Andrews?" I asked, my voice low.

"Jughead." Mr. Andrews scratched his head. He stood up, looked at me, then sat back down again. "Jug. I didn't . . . honestly, I thought you knew. After your mom left, your dad's drinking spiraled. You must have noticed. He hardly ever showed up for work. When he did, he was too drunk to function. I had to let him go, Jug."

"When?" I asked, struggling to keep my voice from cracking.

"When . . . ?"

"When did you *fire* him?" The word felt spiny and thick on my tongue.

"Back in March," Mr. Andrews admitted.

March. So he'd been unemployed for months now. Lying to me. Not to my face, of course. Lying to my face would require face-to-face contact. But instead—

"So, where do *you* think he is?" I asked. "Too embarrassed to come home, to face his only son. Where does my dad go every day?"

"Jughead—" Mr. Andrews started, his voice breaking.

"Answer. The question." I fixated on that mark on the floor, like I could set it on fire if I stared hard enough.

"Jug, you know where he goes. Even if you don't want to admit it."

Finally, finally, I looked up. Mr. Andrews's face had crumpled, wrinkled up in sorrow and regret. I felt my own do the same, my forehead tight and my jaw tense.

"So it's true, then? What that Serpent said today?"

"Serpent?" Mr. Andrews leaned in intently. "Did someone threaten you?"

I waved him away. "It's fine. I'm fine. But tell me: what they said to me, about my dad. It's true?" I swiped the back of my hand against my cheek. I refused to shed a single tear. "He's a Serpent again?"

The color drained from Mr. Andrews's face, telling me everything I needed to know. But he did answer.

"He's a Serpent again," he agreed softly. "But, not just *a* Serpent.

"Jughead"—again, he reached for me, and again, I pulled back—"Jug, he's *the* Serpent.

"He's their leader."

Cam:

The eagle has landed. The coast is clear.

Nick:

Um WTH does that mean? Are we speaking in cartoon-military code now?

Annie:

She's trying to be coy—Ronnie's gone-gone. Left for Barneys after our first text. Something about an assignment for Grace.

Cam:

Ugh, GRACE, of course. Like they're really on a first name basis. I mean, MY mother is besties with Anna Wintour and you don't hear ME calling her Anna like we're buddies. It's called CLASS. She could try some.

Annie:

Her father is Hiram Lodge. I think we all know where Veronica gets her ideas about class from. And whatever the case, she's in for a super rude awakening, and soon. My mom says news about her dad's Ponzi scheme just broke on the Post online.

Nick:

Will it stick, tho? Guy's like Teflon. The only white-collar criminal I've ever heard of with possible ties to the mob. Like every kind of supervillain wrapped up in one.

Annie:

According to the Post, it's looking pretty sticky. Even supervillains have their kryptonite. And even the fattest cats still have only nine lives.

Cam:

Ha, good one. Poor Veronica. Her life's about to go up in flames. I almost feel sorry for her. Wait, no—I totally don't.

Annie:

Ouch, Cameron. Stone cold.

Cam:

Oh, please. Are you forgetting the time she "accidentally" ordered me a size XXL for our spirit squad performance & then pretended she genuinely thought that was my actual size? She gave it to me in front of the entire team and made a whole huge deal about how she just "innocently misread my body type." Like WTAH?

Annie:

Nope, haven't forgotten. Just focused on the time she threw herself at Tommy Whitmore three whole seconds after I confessed I had a crush on him. I wasn't saying "stone cold" was, like, a bad thing. #respect, girlfriend.

Cam:

So what'd she ever do to you, Nicky? As long as we're airing our grievances.

Nick:

I mean, nothing, really. Nothing big. That she hasn't done to anyone else. But she hasn't done anything FOR me . . . or WITH me . . . if u get my drift. And, you know, I'm not into it.

Cam:

So she wouldn't get with you is your big gripe? Ugh, you're such a pig. Why am I even surprised?

Annie:

Who do we know that can be at Barneys in ten? It's bound to be a dumpster fire, and I, for one, want a full report.

Cam:

On it, my darlings . . . I'm heading over in a few. Supposedly they just changed out the pumps display, too—killer stilettos unpacked this morning. If spying on V is uncharitable, then buying something for myself is necessary self-care.

Annie:

You, my friend, are the last of the genteel class.

Cam:

Don't u forget it.

CHAPTER FIFTEEN

VERONICA

Holly Golightly had a theory about retail therapy (though in her case, of course, it was really just window-shopping). She said the only cure for a bad mood was a visit to Tiffany's. Calms those "mean reds" right down, right away. *"Nothing bad could happen there,"* that's what Holly said about Tiffany's. And I know just what she meant.

Except for me, it's Barneys all the way.

I barely had time for the coffee I grabbed from Lalo before I had to grab a car to Barneys.

(*I know.* An *Uber.* Like I'm some kind of peasant. But Mom needed the car—and Andre—for herself, and I wasn't about to argue, knowing how busy she was. Yes, it's true; Veronica Lodge is a martyr at heart.)

Well, if Holly Golightly could "jump in a cab" and head to Tiffany's, then I'd do the same with Barneys. In her case, it was therapy. In mine, it was more than that—it was my job.

But that didn't mean it wasn't also therapeutic.

"The quietness and the proud look of it." That's what Holly said she found so soothing about Tiffany's. And yes, Barneys has that proud look—the iconic red awning, the Simon Doonan windows that raised the bar for retail display everywhere. Everything white marble beyond the symmetry of the black-framed doors, bright red club chairs punctuating perfectly spaced seating areas for the weary high-end consumer. It is a triumph of geometry, and a true haven of luxury. The fact that I get to come here and call it "work"? Icing on the Momofuku Milk Bar cake.

(Birthday cake, of course. Always birthday cake. And a cake truffle or two, if you're trying to get on my good side.)

I opened the doors with a satisfying *hiss*, a promise that within this space, life beyond ceased. Those of us who'd pierced the majestic veil of the hallowed place had crossed a threshold, securing our places firmly among the *haves*. Even the smell of Barneys was true luxury: lush and expensive and fragrant. Polished wood and eau de parfum. Blank-faced mannequins posed like hipster outcast props from the set of *A Clockwork Orange*, swathed in chunky wools and creamy cashmeres despite the unrelenting heat of midsummer. In here, seasons ceased to exist, of course. In here, it was utopia, always.

The jewelry case beckoned—a new Jennifer Meyer line of tasseled pendants had "girls' night at Cielo" written all over it—but this trip wasn't about me.

(Oh, who are we kidding? I could—and I *would*—make it about me. But I'd take care of my errand first. That much responsibility, I could handle.)

Women's couture was on the fourth floor, so I reluctantly forced myself past a drool-worthy display of killer embellished stilettos and toward the escalator. Elena, one of my favorite sales associates, was passing by at that exact moment with a rack of candy-colored silk dresses that fluttered like fairy wings with the movement.

"Hey, girl!" I said, waving. "*Gorg*. I'm running to grab some props for the magazine, but promise me you'll set aside one of those for me. Purple, obviously." (It *is* the color of royalty, after all.)

She stopped in her tracks—but reluctantly. "Oh, um, I'm taking these to be steamed . . ." she stammered, her face turning an alarming shade of pink. "The thing is, I don't know when they're going out to the floor."

I frowned. I mean, I was 50 percent kidding when I asked her to put one on hold for me, after all. But even if I wasn't, was *she*? Everyone knows how it works here: I ask for what I want, and then I get it.

It's really very simple.

Or at least, it should be.

I pretended not to read her tone. "Great!" I chirped. "Steam the purple one first. You can leave it for me at the counter." I gave her my brightest smile, the one perfected by monthly laser-whitening treatments.

Her jaw tightened and her shoulders crept up to her ears. Even as she turned away from me, I could read her expression perfectly via body language alone. Something was most definitely up.

Well, forget her. I could care less about her body language.

My first mistake was in even asking, I thought, stepping onto the escalator in a slight huff. What did I care about her tight shoulders and her stupid blunt lob that was two seasons out of date?

Never ask. That's what Daddy always said. *Tell.*

I'd *tell* her the purple dress was mine.

∧∧∧

Lucinda—Grace's personal connection at Barneys—was waiting for me at the top of the escalator next to an enormous garment bag. With the stairs rising up on their mechanized belt to meet her, it was like something out of a superhero movie. Her mass of auburn curls had been pinned into submission with a pair of black enameled chopsticks that I knew for a fact were not meant for eating at all, and, in fact, retailed for more than most people will spend on an upscale serving of Peking duck at Mr. Chow. She cut a striking figure in wide-leg white jeans and a mesh navy crop top over a sequined red bandeau bra—getting in theme for the holiday, I presumed. I recognized her plastic platform sandals from the Prada Spring lookbook and made a mental note to snag a pair of my own before going home this afternoon.

(In a different color. A little individuality goes a long way.)

"Perfect timing!" I exclaimed, stepping gracefully off the top escalator step. "That must be for Her Lady of Divine Grace," aka our personal nickname for Grace around the office. (Never to her face, of course—though I didn't think she would actually mind.)

"It is," Lucinda said, stepping away from the rack for a minute to re-pin her hair so wobbly corkscrews twirled in every direction. "Be careful to hold it upright *at all times*; it's a linen blend that's murder to steam." She looked more stern than the comment actually warranted, given that we were talking about the care and keeping of an article of clothing. A cripplingly expensive article of clothing, sure, but still.

A feeling came over me then. It was that sensation you have when you walk into a room and realize that the people in it were *just* talking about you—and for sure not saying nice things. Or the vibe of someone flashing you stank face from across a crowded auditorium. It was the feeling of being . . . *observed* . . . and not in a positive light. It made my skin tingle, like a light sunburn. When you added that to the awkward way that Cam and Annie had behaved at Lalo, and that vibe I'd had in the Dakota lobby this morning, the feeling went from light sunburn to radiation exposure.

It was definite: Something was going on.

I decided to test the waters, to gauge just exactly how paranoid I was being. "Can I take a peek?" I asked, reaching for the garment bag. Normally, this wouldn't be an issue; not only does Veronica Lodge know how to handle fine clothing but, as discussed, Veronica Lodge also has an overwhelming tendency to get what she wants.

But not this time; Lucinda snatched the bag back so quickly you'd think *I* was radioactive. Her face contorted into an involuntary sneer. "Stop!"

I must have looked shocked, because she took a moment to compose herself, and tried again. "It's just . . . I spent *hours* on it this morning. I'd really rather not risk it getting messy before it gets to Grace."

I *tsk-tsked* her. "And here I thought our relationship was one built on trust!"

It was *not* the winning argument. Now she fully scowled at me, apparently having reached her breaking point. "A Lodge talking about *trust*," she hissed. "That's cute. But the answer is still no."

The blood rushed to my cheeks. "Just what are you insinuating, Lucinda?"

She snorted. "Oh, I think you know. Unless you're still playing the 'plausible deniability' game when it comes to your darling father?"

I took a step closer to her. "I shouldn't have to remind you that my *darling father* is a VIP client at this establishment. Meaning that you would do well to watch your tone."

"Hiding behind him isn't going to do you any good anymore, Veronica," Lucinda said. For a second, it looked like she almost pitied me. "The game is up, princess."

I wanted to shove her, to get in her face and cause her actual, lasting physical violence. But among other things, Daddy always told me not to leave a trail of evidence. So instead, I took the deepest breath imaginable. Then I demanded to speak to her manager.

Lucinda shrugged. "Suit yourself." She tapped a pager clipped to her hip pocket. "I've already contacted her. She's on her way."

Sure enough, seconds later, a manager arrived. It was someone I didn't know, which was unusual enough—I thought I knew *everyone* on the Barneys payroll. Also unusual: the fact that she was looking me up and down like I was a creature at the zoo, something subhuman to be viewed from behind a glass wall or bars—if at all.

"Ms. Lodge," the woman began. "I'm Tamsin Payne—"

"Please. As if I care," I said, cutting her off. "More important than your name is that you talk to your employees about how they treat their most valued customers. Lucinda here was showing me just a little more attitude than I appreciate."

"*Hmm.*" This Tamsin Payne—a made-up moniker by a backwater transplant if I'd ever heard of one—didn't seem very impressed by the news. She swept a jet-black curtain of hair back off her shoulder. "To be honest, Ms. Lodge," she said, "I've been observing you since you came into the store—"

At the mention of being under observation, I whirled around, searching for the hidden cameras that I knew were there, but also knew I'd never find.

"That's illegal, you know," I shot at her, not knowing if that was true, but suspecting it probably was not. Then again, maybe she didn't know that. "*Intimidation is 70 percent bluster,*" Daddy always said. Carry yourself with authority, and people will buy whatever you're (metaphorically) selling.

Except, it didn't seem to be working very well right now. Tamsin held up a hand to cut me off. "I've been observing you since you came in, and frankly, it's you who's been rude and short-tempered with my staff. This is, of course, not appropriate for a Barneys customer, and not acceptable."

"What are you *talking* about?" I exploded. "I've barely seen anyone since I walked in, much less interacted with them." I thought for a moment. "Wait, is this because I asked Elena to put aside one of those silk dresses for me? I don't see why that would be an issue. I often get first pick of new shipments. It's never been a problem before."

"There's a first time for everything," she replied.

"This is *absurd*," I sputtered. "It's harassment. Believe me, when my father hears about this, there will be consequences."

"Believe it or not, Ms. Lodge, I'm not too terribly worried about your father and what he might have to say about this. I have a feeling he's going to be . . . well, let's just say, *otherwise occupied*, and soon."

"What's that, now? *Slander?*" I couldn't help it, my voice rose. Shoppers had begun to form a small cluster around us, morbidly curious despite themselves. God, a snot-nosed little private school diva getting dressed down at an NYC retail icon? This was probably the highlight of these athleisure-clad trophy hausfraus' days.

"Ms. Lodge, you're causing a scene."

"*I'm* causing a scene? I'm being treated like a . . . like a . . . well, certainly not like the valued customer I am! You haven't even *begun* to see the type of scene I'm capable of, trust me. This is inexcusable."

"I agree," the manager said calmly. Her hair fell past her shoulders in a smooth, straight sheen. Her clothes were immaculate, and her makeup was barely there but expertly applied. Everything about her screamed "upper hand" and "composure."

Whereas I'd let myself unravel.

I had to get the situation back under control.

"This must all be a misunderstanding," I offered, backtracking. I still wasn't sure what had happened, or how, but I wanted more than anything to de-escalate the situation, and quickly.

"I'm sure it is," the manager agreed. "You can explain it all to our security team. They'll escort you to one of the back offices where you can speak in private."

"Security team? What?" The room began to spin, and a ringing sounded in my ears. Suddenly, I realized I was taking very shallow breaths, like tiny sips of water. Was this anxiety? I guess the benefit of being a Lodge meant I'd never had to experience it before. The room began to blur. I noticed some of the looky-loos assembled were holding up their phones, making sure to capture every moment of this humiliation.

"I've already called them," she said, and I saw that she had; there they were: two discreetly well-muscled men in black-on-black, headsets framing their sturdy jawlines. It was instantly clear that these men were *not* messing around.

"I don't understand," I said, my voice sounding very small and far away. "What . . . ? How did this happen?" I'd come into Barneys today the way I came into Barneys every day; where was the wrong turn taken? My eyes filled with hot tears. How was I going to explain this to my parents? Being questioned by security like a common criminal?

How was I going to get out of it, at all?

Because one thing was suddenly crystal clear:

Whatever power I'd thought I wielded here, whatever clout I perceived myself to have—it was gone. Long gone. And looking at the linebacker types forming a wall in front of me, it didn't look like I'd be getting it back anytime soon.

"I'll . . . come with you," I stammered, reluctant. "To talk. But I'll need to contact my father. And his lawyer. Immediately."

The smaller of the two guards stepped forward and placed a firm hand on my elbow. He wasn't rough—but he definitely wasn't gentle. "Watch it," I said—but with way less venom than my usual.

"We'll do our best to get in touch with your father and his lawyer, Ms. Lodge," Tamsin said sweetly. "I have to warn you, though—they're probably both otherwise occupied right now."

"What would you know about my father's lawyer?"

Seriously, what?

"Miss Lodge . . . well, I'm guessing you haven't seen the *Post* yet today. Online. *Page Six* notification."

Before I could respond, the guards guided me past the growing circle of camera phones and down a long hall, my vision tunneling to the double doors ahead as my thoughts raced.

All my life, there'd been something, some secret knowledge of what it meant to be a pampered, spoiled princess—the underlying sense that somewhere, there was another shoe. And that someday, somehow, the other shoe would drop. A moment of reckoning, even if I wasn't sure for *what*.

Had that moment finally arrived?

"Most kings get their heads cut off." That was from a Basquiat work I saw at a Whitney retrospective last spring. At the time, it seemed subversive, whimsical. But right now, with the possibility of Daddy being useless to assist me, it felt downright prophetic.

A princess could have her head cut off, too.

The bigger they are, the harder they fall. That was another saying, right? Some rap song I danced to at 1 Oak, freshman year?

The double doors opened with a pneumatic hiccup, and then my mind went blank for a bit.

BREAKING VIA *TMZ*:

**for EXCLUSIVE VIDEO of Uptown girl
VERONICA LODGE getting carted off by security
at Barneys! What would Daddy say? Or is he too
busy with scandals of his own?**

POLL:

Does Veronica Lodge deserve to be
taken down a peg? Y/N

○ YES, bitch has got to go down! **81%**

○ NO, like attracts like, so I'll, like, keep my
energy clean and pure, TYVM. **15%**

○ WHO'S VERONICA LODGE AND WHY
SHOULD I CARE? **4%**

CHAPTER SIXTEEN

ARCHIE

One surefire way to combat any ideas that your father's playing favorites with you at your work site is to be everybody's guy Friday, basically a glorified lackey. Not that I minded, since it meant a break from pouring concrete, and generally Dad let me use his truck for quick errands. Maybe it wasn't technically 100 percent legal, but no one around here was gonna give Fred Andrews a hard time about that. Sheriff Keller and my Dad were drinking buddies, for Pete's sake. And I was always super careful on the road. That was me to a T: Archie Andrews, Solid Citizen. I wondered sometimes if that would be the epigraph they'd etch on my gravestone.

No wonder I'd been looking for a little excitement, a little something new, when Geraldine came along and tapped into this whole creative side of myself I'd never even guessed was there.

Of all things, we were running short on rolls of fiberglass insulation—so unlike my Dad to run short, it just proved my theory that he had as much on his mind as I did, if not more. Lenny gave me a sheet with the exact specs we'd need and off I went. "Don't loiter," he warned, like hanging around the hardware store on Main was my idea of a party.

"I'll be quick," I promised. Meaning it.

The ride into town reminded me of that first time, with Geraldine—well, she was still Ms. Grundy to me, then. The first time she was a woman and I was a guy rather than student and teacher, I mean. Me walking along the shoulder of the road, roasting through my tank top in the summer sun. Her pulling over in that cute little Bug that said so much more about her personality than I might have guessed based on music class alone. Those heart-shaped sunglasses that made her seem less like a teacher and more like someone I . . . well, more like someone who was right for me.

Which was true, and also not completely true.

It had only been a few weeks since that fateful day, but everything—everything!—felt different.

Most of the differences were good.

No—most of them were *great*.

∿∿∿

As Lenny predicted, it didn't take long to find the insulation I needed at the hardware store. I picked up double what Dad was asking for just to be safe. I was glad to be an easy customer; Dilton Doiley was in there in his full Adventure Scout getup, pushing the clerk to sell him bullets for his pellet gun. The clerk wasn't having it, not even when Dilton whipped out a *signed note from his father* like we were in grade school or something. Except the only guns I played with in grade school were squirt guns, and those never required any special permission.

"It's standard issue for the Scouts," Dilton was saying, his jaw clenched so tight I thought his head was gonna explode.

"Then come back with an actual Scout Leader. One who's over eighteen," the clerk said over Dilton's attempts to protest.

"The clearing by Striker's Cove is plenty safe," the clerk went on. "Your worst danger down there is of drowning. But then, you'd know that—being a true Scout and all."

Dilton glared but didn't say anything.

"You shouldn't need weapons. The bears will stay away as long as you know your food storage."

"Of course I do."

"Well, good, then. You've got nothing to worry about," the clerk said. "You bring a gun down there with you, you're more likely to hurt yourself or one of your own. I shouldn't have to tell you that, son."

"Thanks for the lecture," Dilton grumbled. He stuffed a wallet into his back pocket. "Remind me not to bother with this place again. I can figure out a way to get what I need elsewhere." He stormed off.

"I sure hope you don't!" the clerk said cheerfully. To me he said, "That boy's wound too tight. One more reason he shouldn't be needing a gun."

"Yeah," I said noncommittally, not really wanting to get into it. Dilton Doiley and his Scouts weren't my concern— except for the fact that they'd be camping by Striker's Cove tonight, apparently.

Which meant that Geraldine and I would have to find a clearing far enough away from them that there'd be no chance of our being spotted.

It wasn't an unsolvable problem, but it was a new wrinkle, and it was all I was thinking about as I left the store, giving the clerk enough of a wave so as not to be rude.

I was caught up enough in my own thoughts that I managed to crash directly into Valerie Brown, one-third of Josie and the Pussycats. She was pretty preoccupied herself, hunched over her phone and squinting intently.

"Whoa," I said, stepping back as quickly as I could. "Sorry about that. Didn't mean to trample you."

"What? No, it was my bad," she said, her voice soft. Her eyes were a hazel that changed color as the sunlight played off her face. "Texting and walking—bad call. I'm not coordinated enough for that."

"What's going on? You looked pretty . . . serious, there," I said. "I mean, not to pry." I didn't know Val that well, but I had mad respect for her musical skills, even more so now that I was getting into playing music of my own. Or, you know, trying to.

She shrugged. "So stupid. Band drama. Or maybe not even, I don't know. We're just getting our set list together, and making plans for tonight—"

"Wait, you don't all go home early and drink, like, tea with lemon the night before a big gig so you can be fresh and rested?"

Val burst out laughing. "That is *definitely* not the Pussycats' way. We like to roar—you know, go 'claws out.' It's the best way I know of to settle any preshow jitters."

"Better than that old thing about, you know, picturing the audience in their underwear?"

She gave me a look. "Archie, I don't think anyone really does that." And she was probably right, but then there was an uncomfortable beat where I'm pretty sure we were each thinking about the other one's underwear, even though we *really* didn't want to.

"Hang on," she started, and I almost burst into an apology for having an involuntary thought, but before I could, she pointed, clarifying what it was that had caught her attention. "That's weird."

It took me a second to figure out just what she was pointing out, because it was two figures a block away, partially hidden by a large oak tree.

"Isn't that . . . like, Jughead's dad? He's a Serpent, right?" Val asked.

"FP's not a Serpent," I corrected her. "I mean, okay, technically. But in name only. He went through a rough patch, but he cleaned up his act. He's working for my dad now, you know."

Val looked at me. "Archie," she pointed out, "if FP Jones is working for your father, then why isn't he, you know . . . *working for your father*?"

"I . . ." I didn't know what to say. The conversation that Dad and I'd had at lunch came back to me like a voiceover in a cheesy movie—he was glad I'd be staying at Jughead's because . . . but he never said why.

He never said why because he didn't want to admit it— what happened, really, between him and FP. He didn't want to admit that FP *didn't* get clean, didn't pull away from the Serpents the way he'd had Jughead believe.

"I'm an idiot," I said, the weight of it hitting me like a body blow.

Val put a hand on my arm. Her skin was surprisingly soft.

"You're not an idiot. You just prefer to give people the benefit of the doubt. Honestly, it's a good thing. And it's in rare supply these days."

I was startled by how nice she was being, the kind things she was saying to me, about me. Everyone knows the Pussycats are fierce and talented and gorgeous as hell, but I'd never really taken a beat to *notice* Val.

But now, I couldn't help it. She was right there. And it was . . . nice.

"Does Jug know about his dad, do you think?" she asked.

I shook my head. "I doubt it." And I *did* doubt it—but I couldn't be sure. Because we didn't hang out anymore. Because of Geraldine.

And that was what it all came down to, wasn't it? Geraldine. Here was Val. There was FP. And Jughead was around, somewhere, and he could probably use a friend. But I had . . . plans. And no matter how much I liked to think of myself as the good guy, those plans were my priority.

Val's phone buzzed again, breaking the momentary spell between us. She flicked her gaze at it, then sighed. "Reggie Mantle is nothing if not persistent," she grumbled.

I thought of Reggie's texts from earlier in the day. "That's an understatement." I laughed.

"He wants us to play some gig in New York City," she said. "Tomorrow. Like, after our set at Town Hall."

"What? That's amazing!" I couldn't help it—I reached out

and grabbed her by the shoulders. "You have to do it! The City—that's the dream!"

"I know, right? But I'm not sure it's Josie's dream is the thing." She shrugged. "Daddy issues."

Josie's dad was a famous jazz musician who dominated the downtown music scene in New York by his own right. You'd think that would make Josie *more* eager to prove herself there.

But there was FP, lying to Jughead about how he was spending his days. And my father, keeping the truth of his partnership with FP a secret. We all have our parent issues, I guess. Nobody knows what's going on with anyone else, truly. I was in no position to comment on Josie's decisions.

I took Val by the wrist and looked her in the eyes. "Well," I said, "I hope it works out for you. But, you know, you guys are crazy talented. This won't be your only shot."

She blinked. Her eyelashes were full like an anime character's. "Thanks, Andrews. That's sweet of you to say. I hope you come to the show tomorrow."

"Of course," I said automatically. Then I remembered my plans with Geraldine. I didn't actually know how long our date would go on. I only knew that I'd never be the one to cut it short. "I'll definitely try."

I'll try. It was looking to be my new mantra. But was it enough?

From: HLodge@LodgeIndustries.net
To: Fred@AndrewsConstruction.com
Re: Old acquaintance

Hello Fred,

I suppose it's a cliché to say, "Long time, no see," but what do you say, instead, when that happens to be the truth? In any case, I hope you're well, and that you're happy enough to hear from me despite our . . . well, our rocky past.

I wish I could say this was just a friendly check-in—I can just hear you now, going on about how there's always an ulterior motive with a Lodge. And in this case, unfortunately, it's the truth. You see, I may be back in town again, and soon. Very soon, if the whisperings here among the Manhattan elite are to be believed. (There are always whisperings; it's the veracity of the rumors that needs cautious scrutiny.)

It's Hiram, just as you always suspected it would be. I suppose he wasn't always as careful as he claimed he was being. And yes, you can say, "I told you so," if you promise not to gloat too badly.

Needless to say, he'll probably be going away for a time. I probably don't need to say more than that, do I? In which case there's a good chance I'll find myself back in my old stomping grounds—*our* old stomping grounds. Riverdale. I'm sure you have some thoughts about that.

There are a lot of things I could tell you I'll need: a job, a source of income, some kids my daughter's age to show her the ropes at Riverdale High. (Although, if I'm being honest, she'll probably be running the school in a week, who am I kidding?) And I guess I am, however obliquely, asking for those things now.

But most of all, what I'd love—even if I don't, truly, deserve it—is your friendship. I'm hoping that after all this time, after everything that's happened . . .
Well, I'm really hoping that it's not too much to ask.

With love,
Hermione

[Delete]

PART III: EVENING

CHAPTER SEVENTEEN

BETTY

Dear Diary:

Finally, *finally*, Cleo and Rebecca went home for the evening. I always thought 5 p.m. was the end of a business day. But the news cycle on a blog never really stops, so believe it or not, that was pretty early for them. Rebecca must've thought I was crazy for sticking around, or maybe they both thought I was sucking up, trying to prove a point.

"It's a *holiday*, Betty," Rebecca said, like she hadn't just spent the whole afternoon posting articles on nail polish trends and the latest in home décor, as if it were any other day of the week. "And when I said I was going to forget about the closet thing and give you another chance, I meant it. You don't have to stay all night to prove something to me."

"Thanks," I said, feeling a weird mix of gratitude that she was being cool, and fury at having been set up in the first place.

"What, don't you have somewhere to be?" Cleo asked in a faux-concerned tone. Like she was sure that I didn't and wanted to be certain that Rebecca knew it, too. Poor lame, sad, un-hip Betty from Podunk little Riverdale, and with no cool LA friends to speak of.

She *had* to be the one who framed me. No question. But it was okay now. Because I was going to prove it.

I shot Cleo a smug little smile. "I have dinner plans," I told them, "but my date is finishing some stuff up of his own. He'll be here soon. It's no big. You guys go. I'll lock up." Cleo probably thought I was making my date up. Again: I didn't care.

"Thanks, Betty. Sorry that Lodge girl was so hard to track down. I really appreciate the write-up you prepped." At least I finally did seem to be on Rebecca's good side, in spite of the day's drama.

"Of course. Anytime." I gave them both a wave. "Have a great holiday!"

"You too," Rebecca said, while Cleo gave a more non-committal murmur, hot on her Charlotte Olympia platform heels. (See? LA Betty WAS picking *some* things up.)

I set a timer on my phone when they left to count down a full ten minutes. I figured that was a safe enough buffer.

As the numbers ticked down, I paced the space, randomly stopping to straighten a book on a color-coded shelf, or fan out a magazine display more neatly.

I counted the number of green apples in the kitchen fruit bowl (six), and the number of red (three), then spent a few minutes wondering if that was the typical ratio we kept on hand, or if people just preferred red to green. Then I spent a few minutes wondering why I was wasting my time wondering about that.

When my phone timer finally chirped, it was like a bomb going off in my stomach. And I mean that in a good way, believe it or not. I jumped, and shut the alarm off so that it was quiet and still in the office again. All I could hear was the sound of my own breathing.

All those years reading Nancy Drew stories like they were textbooks—it wasn't for nothing. Yeah, I didn't get the chance to break into Cleo's phone. She guards that tighter than most people hold their Social Security numbers. But when I was snapping pictures of her desk earlier, I'd managed to catch one thing, almost unintentionally . . .

Her employee pass.

At the time, it seemed borderline useless. Great, what was I going to do, log her in and out of the building? That would be helpful if I were trying to frame her for something, but (for now, at least) that wasn't the plan.

It wasn't until I was at my desk a half hour or so later that it dawned on me. Another, better use for the pass.

"Make sure you log off before you leave," Rebecca told me, watching as I pecked away in vain at this non-story about Veronica Lodge. "Otherwise you won't be able to log on remotely and finish the article later, if it comes to that."

"Yep." I said it absentmindedly, on autopilot, still fixated on how to pull a compelling profile out of absolute thin air. But then the full impact of her words hit me:

Our office was mostly made up of freelancers, temps, and interns—transients who didn't have dedicated space in the office. Unlike Rebecca, who, of course, had her own office, we were relegated to playing musical chairs at the numerous "floater" desks scattered throughout the bullpen. That meant that in order to ensure the security of our data, we each had to log into a computer specifically if we wanted to use it.

And our login code was printed on our employee pass.

I had Cleo's employee pass, ergo, I had access to her whole online history at *Hello Giggles*.

Respectful? Not so much. But turnabout is fair play.

I checked my phone: 5:20 p.m. Brad would be here soon. But I could work quickly. A few keystrokes was all it took to get into Cleo's system. HELLO, her screen welcomed me.

(It was the warmest greeting I'd received since starting at *Hello Giggles*, now that I thought about it. How lame was that?)

Her files were a mess—a jumble of story ideas and half-baked pitches that I knew from being at the editorial meetings she'd never even bothered to bring up. The desktop painted a different picture than the sleek, composed girl I imagined her to be. This Cleo was a frustrated wannabe writer, stuck behind the reception desk the same way I was stuck in filing.

In truth, in another universe, we should have been friends. We could've been allies for each other. But some people aren't built that way. If this were a reality show, Cleo'd be the one saying she didn't come here to make friends.

Which was fine. She hadn't. Too bad for her.

If her document files told me she was a frustrated writer, her emails told me she was a social-climbing striver who just couldn't get a foothold. So many back and forths with Rebecca about an upcoming event for . . . Toni Morrison!

Cleo had good ideas for the event: She knew a caterer who'd give a fair price, she communicated with the event space and was super professional with Toni Morrison's publisher and her publicist. I hated to admit it, but she was handling all the organization like a pro.

(I mean, I *really* hated to admit it. It felt like this gig should have been mine to lose.)

But then, buried ten emails deep in a multiperson, upper-staff thread, I saw it:

betty cooper to be assigned as ms. morrison's on-site handler?

Written by Rebecca herself. I blinked and read the sentence three more times—once out loud, for good measure.

It turns out, Rebecca had taken note of me, somehow, even if she hadn't made it known before today. She'd seen how interested I was in the editorial process—AND she'd noticed that I almost always had a Toni Morrison novel tucked under one arm.

Score one for the Pollyanna girl next door from Podunkville, I thought, satisfied.

Well, now I knew why Cleo was so resentful of me. Too bad for her. In a certain way, I pitied her (but not *that* much, given how she'd been so nasty to me all day for something I had nothing at all to do with in the first place. I'm Betty Cooper, Nice Girl Next Door, not Betty Cooper, Effing Saint.). Cleo was gross, sure, but it was hard to stay too mad at her when I suddenly knew I'd be getting my biggest break yet—and a chance to work with my literary idol!

I logged out of Cleo's system and broke out my phone to text Polly. I knew she'd be thrilled for me. But before I could get the words out, the front door buzzed. Brad was here. Through the glass-paned door, I could see he was holding a bouquet of peonies, my favorite. At the sight of him, I broke into a face-splitting smile. LA Betty was killing it today.

I guessed Polly could wait just a few minutes more.

∿∿∿

I let Brad in and impulsively pulled him in for a monster hug, still a little dizzy from the Toni Morrison reveal. He didn't protest, but he did pull back after a minute, laughing. "Having a good day?" he asked.

"Having the *best* day," I assured him. I amended that. "Well, not the best day. There were moments. But all's well that ends well. And it's all ending pretty darn well." I gave him an appreciative once-over.

"I like the sound of that," he said. "So, what's going on?"

I grabbed him by the wrist and led him to the desk I'd been working at all day. "Well, you know I've been dying to do some actual writing."

"I do know that. But not literally dying."

I raised an eyebrow. "You don't need to correct a writer about the proper use of 'literal' and 'figurative.'"

"You were using the word 'literally' figuratively," he quipped, and he gave such a dopey grin that I laughed and kissed him. "Good Day Betty is fun," he said, kissing me back.

"Fine, whatever. *Anyway*, randomly, today I found Rebecca going over some home décor samples, and after talking for a little bit, she offered me a chance to do a write-up about it."

"Temporary wallpaper?" he guessed.

"Sort of. Also? You're so LA that you would even know that."

"I take that as a compliment. Anyway, show me the piece."

"No! I mean, I will—I can, but the point is: Who even cares about a silly blurb about home trends? Because the thing is, after I wrote that up, she assigned me something bigger— an actual profile."

"Wow! Who?"

I made a face. "Some random NYC socialite named Veronica Lodge. Honestly, I'd never even heard of her."

His eyebrows raised. "Veronica Lodge? Isn't she, like, best friends with Zendaya or something? Weren't they scuba diving in Tulum together over spring break?"

I gave him a look. "Again: so LA. But I'll admit, I'm glad the name means something to you. I mean, it's just a fluff piece, gossip, but—"

"But it's exactly the sort of fluffy gossip that people read," he finished.

"Exactly!"

"So can I see it?"

"Yes. But you have to promise to be nice."

"When am I ever not nice?" he pointed out.

"True." I bit my lip. "I'm just nervous because, well . . . in addition to this being my first big piece, it's been a hard one. She's impossible to track down. So I basically had to piece it together from scraps."

"I'm sure your scraps are amazing," he said, pulling up a chair and settling in front of the monitor. "Now: less talk-y, more read-y."

"Eek." I shivered. "Okay." I logged into the system and found my way into the database where the filed articles lived. *Tap, tap, tap.*

My stomach dropped. My heart sank. My throat went dry.

"Which one is it, Betty?" Brad asked, confused but perky.

Blood rushed in my ears like crashing waves.

"Betty?" Brad asked again, less certain now.

My voice was low and tight: pure, controlled rage. "It's not there," I said. I clenched my hands into fists, ignoring the pain of the broken skin of my palms.

Brad sat up straighter in his chair. "No, that's nuts. Of course it's there. Where would it have gone?"

I closed my eyes. "It was deleted."

"*What?* Why? By who?" Brad leaned in so close his nose was practically touching the monitor, like he could make the file reappear through sheer force of will. "That's . . . Betty, that's super messed up. Are you *sure* it's gone?"

In response, I hunched over the keyboard and expanded the database to show all files. I pounded a search for my article into the keyboard.

It came up blank, of course.

"Who would do that?" Brad asked, mystified.

I ignored him, the pounding in my chest growing more and more intense as I looked through my personal files, desperately searching for a backup of the article.

Obviously, it didn't exist.

Obviously, I'd been so stupidly excited to file my first article, I tossed the original the second the file was saved. I'd never counted on *my own freaking coworker sabotaging me.*

A pent-up cry escaped me and I slammed my fists on the desk. Brad flinched, but I didn't care. The rage, the darkness—it was valid, and what's more, it was part of me. Maybe it was better that he see it now, sooner than later. If he ran, so be it. Everything else was falling apart, anyway.

How many minutes had passed since he'd walked in the door with those peonies? Since I'd thought this was one of my best days in LA yet? Not even twenty. Not even fifteen. Everything had flip-flopped.

Brad put a hand on my arm. Gentle, but in a way that made me feel like a skittish horse he was working carefully to calm. "It's okay, Betty," he said. "It sucks, whatever happened—"

"The article. Was. Deleted."

"Whatever happened," he repeated, "you're a writer, you're a pro. You can fix it. You can write it again. The words are still there—they came from your brain, after all." He tapped at my forehead, trying to be affectionate, but I shrank away.

"Still there? I mean, maybe! But you have no idea how hard it was getting those words down in the first place! I've been chasing this girl all day! And whether or not you want to believe it, someone in the office screwed me over. So not only is the piece gone, but I've got a . . . what? An *archnemesis*? What is this, a comic book or a superhero story?"

"Bright side," he countered. He was trying so hard! "Bright side: You'd have to be one all-powerful superhero to have attracted such an evil archnemesis."

I sighed and crossed my arms over my chest. "That is one hell of a stretch for a bright side." I slumped into the chair next to him and swiveled so we were facing each other.

"So what if we have to postpone dinner? So I can rewrite the article. I just . . . it's such a huge opportunity, and I really don't want to let Rebecca down." There was the Toni Morrison event to think about, among other things, after all.

"We can make it a working dinner," he offered. "I'll grab us pizza."

I almost melted, he was being so sweet. "And you'll just sit here while I'm writing? That's no fun for you."

He held up his phone. "I've got Two Dots. And Netflix. I'm good."

I touched my forehead to his. "You *are* good. The best. And I'll make it up to you."

He waggled an eyebrow at me, teasing. "I like the sound of that."

"Don't be gross." I waved a finger at him. "Well, maybe a *little* dirty is okay." Seeing as how he was currently in the running for Most Amazing Date Ever.

It was enough to make a girl forget about a certain red-headed neighbor some three thousand miles away.

(Or did the mere fact of thinking that mean I *hadn't* forgotten? Whatever—I wasn't going down that rabbit hole right now.)

My phone buzzed. I glance at the incoming message.

And just like that, my blood ran cold all over again.

Flip-flop. It was that kind of day, I guess. One where everything can turn on a dime. In a breath. A heartbeat.

"Betty? You're making that Hulk face again. What's going on?"

I turned to Brad, stony. "That was Rebecca," I told him,

struggling to keep my voice even. "I don't need to rewrite the story. We can go out to eat after all."

He tilted his head curiously. "And yet, it's seeming like this is somehow not the good news one might expect?"

"I don't need to rewrite the story," I explained, so calm and restrained that my organs were quivering, "because it's been killed. They're not running it. They don't want a piece on Veronica Lodge right now, after all. It's been bumped by something bigger."

Something bigger that *I* wasn't going to write.

"Oh man. Betty, that really sucks," Brad said. He reached an arm out to console me. "But there's still a bright side here—you wrote that piece on the, you know, the wall-paper, and your boss is, I guess, ready to start seeing you as a writer—"

"DON'T 'BRIGHT SIDE' ME!" I screamed, deep and primal, loud enough that I startled myself.

Brad gave me a look and inched back. It only infuriated me more.

"Damn it!" I pounded my fists on my desk again, feeling the phone crack in my hands. I threw the phone across the room as hard as I could, watching it smack the window and bounce to the floor.

"Betty." Brad spoke softly again. He took my hand, the one that had slammed the phone. "You're bleeding."

I looked down. I *was* bleeding, bright red rivulets forming road maps along my palm, dripping to the desktop in a macabre spatter.

"There's a first aid kid in the break room," I said numbly.

Brad looked doubtful. "Are you sure? It looks like it might need a stitch or two. Maybe we should go to urgent care just to be safe."

"It's *fine*." Apparently I was insistent enough that he didn't bother to suggest it again. He stood up, presumably to hunt down the first aid kit. But first he picked my phone up where it had landed across the room.

"There's another message," he said, looking at it. "Your sister. I can . . . read it for you?"

"Whatever," I said, too worn out to think about it. "We've been playing phone tag all day. I'll just call her tomorrow."

Today had been nothing but rapid ups and downs, ridiculous drama beyond anything I could possibly have imagined. So whatever it was that Polly was texting about, it could wait.

Whatever it was, it could certainly keep another day.

C Blossom:

The boy isn't cooperating. I'll need you to get Jason to the Whyte Wyrm this evening.

[Unknown ID]:

I can do it . . . . it'll cost a bit more.

C Blossom:

Has your fee been an issue yet? Just get it done.

∿∿∿

[Unknown ID]:

Got one last package for you. Meet at Whyte Wyrm in 30.

Jason:

First drop done, car picked up. Why more now?

∿∿∿

[Unknown ID]:

Whyte Wyrm in 30. Something's up, not sure what yet. Be prepared.

Joaquin [Burner]:

~~~

One last errand for the Serpents. Then all on track.

Polly:

No! I wish it were all over. Promise to be careful! See you soon. Love you so much.

Jason:

It'll be over sooner than you know. I'll be careful. Love you—and the baby—too.

CHAPTER EIGHTEEN

JUGHEAD

Onscreen, an alien mothership with one-fourth the mass of the moon had just entered the Earth's orbit. As you might imagine, the general public was not exactly chill about it. On the one hand, to the casual, rational observer, this made perfect sense. But casual and rational wasn't really where I was at, just then.

My father. Serpent king. No wonder Mom left, no wonder he was drinking . . . and no wonder Fred Andrews had to let him go.

I'm not an idiot. I know that everything that happened to my dad, happened *because* of him. Because of his choices and his behavior. He wasn't some innocent victim.

No, he wasn't innocent. But he was my father, and despite all the rubbish, I still loved him.

So you can see where, for me, the idea of an alien invasion going down was sounding kind of appealing, right about now. It was definitely a potential improvement on my current situation.

I'd been hiding in the projection booth, not wanting to have to interact with actual people, but for once, the small, cramped space actually felt as small and cramped as it was. So I came outside for a breather, only to be immediately reminded of why it is that I go so damn far out of my way to avoid actual people as much as possible.

The lot was packed. *Independence Day* itself wasn't such a big draw, even ironically speaking, but then again, there weren't a ton of other options in terms of Riverdale nightlife. "Independence Eve" at the Twilight was sort of a tradition, like maple syrup or telling campfire stories about Sweetie, the Sweetwater snake monster.

Some people seemed to be having genuine, relaxed fun—over at the front of the lot, I saw Moose and Midge parked with Kevin Keller in their backseat. I guess three isn't always a crowd? They were laughing and tossing popcorn at the screen any time anything cheesy happened, which was basically every four seconds. I'd have to clean up the mess, I knew, but at least some folks were enjoying themselves.

By the concession stand, though, a small crowd had formed. Josie, Val, and Melody were gathered, Pussycat ears in place and T-shirt sleeves rolled up. Josie was passing around a phone for some rubberneckers, one of whom was Cheryl Blossom.

"A new tat? Isn't body art last century's rebellion?" Cheryl was saying.

To her credit, Josie just rolled her eyes. I never did understand why those two were friends, but somehow, it seemed to work. "Scoff all you want, Cheryl, but it's our thing. We Pussycats howl the night before a gig. Sometimes that includes body art, and Val found this amazing sketch that we all agreed on."

"What, is it, like, the Chinese symbol for 'meow'?" Cheryl sneered.

"Jealousy is unbecoming, dear," Josie replied.

"So what's the rest of the plan?" Ethel Muggs was asking shyly.

"Some of it is classified info," Josie told her. "But, you know, we like to raise a little hell. And send a little psych-out message to our opening act so they *know* we're going to blow them off the stage."

"Like last time, we graffitied the door of their practice space—" Melody started, before Josie shut her up with a glare.

"Then there was the time you challenged *me* to a drag race," Reggie said, stepping into the conversation.

"And won." Josie smirked.

"Wanna go again?" he asked.

"You already lost to us once," Josie said. "Sloppy seconds—not my thing."

Reggie's face went rigid. "You know, I've been busting my ass for you all day, trying to line up a gig—a good one! Better than anything you'll get in this stupid little town. And you're just completely ungrateful."

"I don't owe you anything, Mantle," Josie said, stepping forward. "Certainly not gratitude for something I never asked you to do. How many times do I have to tell you: We don't need a manager."

"Enough already, Reggie," Val said, more tempered than Josie was being. "It's obvious you're only doing this because of your feelings for Josie."

"Feelings for Josie? What are you talking about?"

"Come on," Val said, still more kindly than I would have been about it. "It's not like we forgot about that time you made up that story about having a terminal disease, just so Josie would go to the middle school dance with you."

"That was sixth grade!" Reggie sputtered. "And the Josie thing was just a small part of it. I wanted to see how badly I could scam the rest of you. And by the way—pretty badly, was the answer. Wasn't it Ethel who set up an online donation site to collect money for my 'treatments'?"

He sneered at Ethel, who blushed and shrank up into her shirt collar.

"Only a sociopath would do something like that just for fun!" Josie said. "Is it really any huge surprise I wouldn't want you as a manager—*or* as a boyfriend?"

Reggie clenched his jaw. I didn't think he'd hit a girl, but the way he was looking, I wasn't sure. As much as I wanted to stay out of it, I couldn't stay silent.

"Come on, Reggie," I said. "People are just here for the movie. Relax. You don't have to freak out on Josie for wanting to do her own thing."

"Shut up, freak!" he shouted. "Who the hell asked you?"

No one. No one asked me. And yet, I am a glutton for punishment, I thought, walking away from the group.

Cheryl put up her hand. "Reggie, the girls don't have time for this. But believe it or not, this little melodrama is not the center of my universe tonight. There are crises in motion elsewhere, as we speak, that need my attention. So"—she turned to Josie—"beloved companions and"—she glanced at Reggie—"fellow classmates, you'll have to excuse me now. I have elsewhere to be."

She stalked past the crowd, signature red boots cutting a swath like a warning sign. Very deliberately, she stomped directly into Polly Cooper, who was waiting in line for popcorn with some of her cheerleader friends. "Be gone, she-devil," Cheryl hissed. "Jay-Jay is finally free of you, and I'm thinking the rest of us deserve the same privilege."

Polly just shook her head. "I'm going to give Betty one last try," she said to her friends, and moved to a quieter corner farther from the movie screen. "Don't worry about Jason and me," she said to Cheryl as she walked off.

"Don't worry, I'm not!" Cheryl called after her, irate.

With no one left to focus her anger on, she turned to me. "Don't you have a bridge to be sniveling under, troll?" she spat. I ignored her, thinking it was finally time to go back to my "cozy" projection booth. There was a reason I'd come up with my whole "hard pass on other people" stance, even if I sometimes temporarily forgot about it.

As I turned to go, though, Reggie grabbed me. His fingers dug into my shoulder as he pulled me around. "The lady is talking to you, freak," he said.

"Thanks, but I don't need a translator," I told him. "Especially not a mouth-breather who barely has a handle on the English language."

"You don't talk to me that way," Reggie growled. He shoved me, hard, so I went back into the concession stand. Immediately, there was a rush of reaction—people calling out, that little zing in the air just before everyone goes completely ape—but right away, his Bulldog lapdogs pulled him back. "*It's* not worth it," one of them said, meaning me—*I* wasn't worth it. I wasn't offended.

"You got lucky, Jones," Reggie called as I pulled myself together and went back to the projection room.

Yeah. Lucky.

That's just how I would have described it myself.

∿∿∿

There was a phone in the projection room, an old rotary model that you wouldn't have thought worked, but it did. We weren't really supposed to use it unless it was an emergency, but even if this wasn't *actually, technically* an emergency, it suddenly felt like my entire world was imploding.

I dialed slowly. I knew the number by heart, even though it was a fairly new one. It rang for what felt like years. I was just about to hang up when I heard the *click* of someone picking up on the other line. That *click* just then—it felt like a lifeline.

"Hello?"

Jellybean's voice sounded different—deeper, a little more mature, even though, of course, she hadn't really been gone long enough for that to be the case. Still, my own voice cracked when I spoke, and I struggled to keep it together, to be calm. "Hey," I said, the word wavering. "It's me."

"Jughead!" She sounded so happy to hear from me, it almost made up for the mountain of trash that'd been sliding downhill toward me since the second I woke up this morning. "How are you?"

"I'm—good." I forced the lie out. She didn't need the full extent of my reality. "What's going on in Toledo, Jellybean?"

"It's just JB now," she said, indignant. "Jellybean's *so* immature."

I smiled to myself. "Is that so?"

"Mom's not home," she said abruptly. "Like, if you wanted to ask her something specific. But you can tell me!" she chirped. "I'm good at giving messages."

Do you miss me? Are you coming home? Can I come to you? What should I do about Dad?

What am I going to do?

No, I didn't have a specific question for my mother. She wasn't going to solve this for me, couldn't solve this for me. If she could've, she would have taken me with her when she left.

"Tell me about the friends you're making, *JB*," I said. I settled back in the rickety old chair in the room and listened to her go on, prattling away in that hyper-detailed way that kids do. While she talked, I took a good look around the projection room—the interior footprint, the electrical outlets, what sort of furniture could be shoved to one side to make room for a sleeping bag . . . if need be.

It could work, I decided. It would have to work.

I'd pack a bag and bring it over later tonight, after the movie, once the place had cleared out. I doubted anyone would figure me out.

In order for someone to figure me out, they'd have to be paying attention in the first place.

"Are you listening, Juggie?"

"I am, JB," I promised. "Keep talking."

From: CBlossom@MapleFarm.net
To: HLodge@LodgeIndustries.net
Re: No Subject

My dear, after all this time, it pains me to send you this warning—
your husband's time has come. I've taken the liberty of including a link to the story that the *Times* will be breaking in just a
few moments.

From: HLodge@LodgeIndustries.net
To: CBlossom@MapleFarm.net
Re: No Subject

Your sympathies are duly noted, Clifford. As are your loyalties—or lack thereof, I should say. Don't for a minute make the mistake of thinking that this is the end. And don't underestimate my husband—or me.

Away from home for a while?
Come home to us.
Allow us to pamper you in style at

The Pembrooke.

———◆———

Known for its impeccable service, timeless décor, and attention to detail, the Pembrooke is one of Rockland County's preeminent boutique hospitality options.

We have a range of booking packages to ensure that you find the optimal lodging for your extended stay. Our lodgings offer space, amenities, and best of all—that personal touch.

To learn more, simply click <u>request information</u>, and a reservation specialist will be in touch soon to assist you.

———◆———

NAME OF APPLICANT: Hermione Lodge
ESTIMATED ARRIVAL DATE: ASAP
ESTIMATED DURATION OF STAY: TBD

CHAPTER NINETEEN

VERONICA

To my absolute dismay (and chagrin), the nonsense at Barneys managed to take up my entire afternoon. After I was escorted to some secret military-torture-style closet of doom, no fewer than three separate security guards and one manager (Tamsin—who, it must be said, did not get any more pleasant with time) descended on me like locusts. It was incredible— they were treating me like a common criminal when, hilariously, the worst thing I'd done since arriving at the store was *ask to buy some of their merchandise with actual money.*

Honestly, one wondered how they treated legitimate criminals!

Anyway, there was an hour or so of berating me for the so-called "attitude" I took with the employees, which I suppose went on for longer than it should have because apparently I wasn't contrite enough.

(Of course I wasn't contrite enough! There was nothing to apologize for! And I'm hardly the easily intimidated type.)

At last, I suppose, Tamsin had had enough of her little power play (maybe something actually pressing arose somewhere else in the store, for once?), and they deigned to let me go. I assured them they'd be hearing from Daddy's lawyers, and they laughed.

I can't recall when else I've experienced such deplorable customer service in my life.

I insisted on buying the purple silk dress—not that they deserved to take any of my family's hard-earned money, but at this point it felt like I should be getting *something* positive out of this whole horrendous experience. I'd already had to text *Vogue* and let them know I wouldn't be able to come by with the props.

(They were oddly understanding about it, I have to say.)

And that should have been the end of it.

Except, it wasn't.

"I'm sorry, Ms. Lodge, but this card has been declined," the salesclerk told me when she tried to ring me up. She held my black American Excess card by one corner, like it was infectious or covered in poison.

"That's not possible." That card has a six-figure spending limit, and not even *I* had done that much damage this month. "Run it again."

She rolled her eyes and swiped the card—aggressively, like

the whole thing was a performance for me. The register gave a little *beep* of protest. She smirked at me. "Declined."

"There must be something wrong," I snapped, grabbing the card back from her. I gave her my Vista instead, and then MasterClass.

Beep. Beep. Smirk. Smirk. *"I'm sorry, Ms. Lodge."*

"I'm sure you are," I hissed, gathering my cards back and stuffing everything into my Louis Vuitton bucket bag.

"When I come back—*if* I come back—you will be gravely sorry for how you've mistreated me."

"Have a nice day," she said impassively.

∧∧∧

So it was most unexpected that I found myself slinking home just in time to make a slight-but-dramatically-late entrance to our own party, the one I was meant to have been helping set up. I'd texted Mom, of course, to let her know I was held up, but she hadn't replied. To me, that said she was beyond furious. My phone ran out of juice the second after I texted her, too, so I couldn't take an Uber or Lyft, and I didn't want to run the risk of my credit cards being declined in a yellow cab. I'd had to *walk* home—and I hadn't had a chance to check out the *Post*, either.

Nigel at the courtyard gate gave me a terse nod—polite, but only minimally so. Feeling completely out of sorts, I

247

marched as proudly as I could to our building. Andre in the lobby had been replaced by Christopher, it having been *literally the duration of his shift* that I'd been detained at Barneys.

"Hello," I said to him, trying to sound brighter than I was feeling. "Fashionably late to my own party—egregious, I know. Do you think I can get away with claiming I like to make an entrance?"

"Of course, Ms. Lodge," Christopher said, keeping his eyes fixed at some indeterminate point on his desk.

"It was a joke," I said, that prickly feeling creeping up along my skin again.

"Of course, Ms. Lodge," he said, utterly toneless. "Ha."

It was the most chilling attempted laugh I'd heard outside of a Stanley Kubrick movie.

To the left, I saw Nicola Mavis, who lived one floor below us, collecting her mail. She was in palazzo pants—silk, but still casual, and bare feet, which seemed odd given that she normally attended our parties.

"Will we be seeing you in a bit?" I asked her. Apparently I startled her, because she jumped.

She turned to me. "Oh," she said. "Veronica. I . . . haven't been up there yet."

"It's okay," I smiled. "Me neither. We can be each other's alibis."

I was joking—obviously—but her response was strained.

"Yes," she said. "I'll be up there soon."

But she didn't sound very convincing.

I took the elevator up to our penthouse, extremely worried about what on earth would be waiting for me when I got there.

∿∿∿

The first thing I noticed when the paneled elevator doors slid open was an eerie silence. We'd hired a jazz trio and yes, in theory they were meant to be subdued, conversation-enhancing, low-decibel, and chill, but this wasn't *chill*. This was *nothing*.

In fact, the feel of the entire foyer as I crept forward, my heart quickening in my throat, was one of suspended animation. The air was heavy, tense, not at all lighthearted like you'd expect of a big holiday bash. The guests were here, gathered—there was one of the Vanderbilt heiresses in a corseted Gabbana that she could barely pull off, the poor dear—but they were silent, like they were collectively holding their breaths.

My goal was to sneak through the kitchen and down the back hallway to the servant's quarters, where I could creep to my bedroom undetected for a quick change. But that wasn't how it ended up playing out.

"M'hija!" It was my father, his voice booming, betraying none of the bizarre tone of the space. "Come here, please." He was calling to me from his office.

"Of course, Daddykins." I stepped lightly, like the room was trip-wired, for reasons I couldn't quite explain to myself. Yes, the guests were here, assembled, but they were still, shell-shocked, frozen, almost like museum dioramas—here was one clutching a glass of Sancerre with the white-knuckled intensity of an Olympic athlete, here was a mini lobster roll being dangled halfway between plate and open mouth, like the intended guest had forgotten his original plan to actually eat it. There was the jazz trio, assembled, as always, adjacent to the fireplace, the French doors thrown open to the summer air. But their instruments were still.

The servers, too, were huddled like mannequins, lined up against the far wall of the hallway in their white shirts and black pants like the world's most overdressed, most passive army.

Every single gaze in the apartment was trained on me as I made my way to Daddy's office. There were Cam, Nick, and Annie—their own faces inscrutable, suffused with several competing expressions that I couldn't, in the moment, unpack.

"Daddy," I said, willing my voice to be strong, "it's so weird out there, did something happen? Did I miss a news flash or something while I was out? Maybe something in the *Post?* And—oh, I have to tell you about the horrendous abuse I suffered at Barneys. It's been—"

I stopped.

I dropped my bag. It skidded off my open-toed shoes, which should have hurt, or at least made me blanch, but I was so shocked at the sight in front of me that I didn't so much as blink.

If the rooms outside were crowded—with murmuring, waxwork party-goers—then this room was electric. It was standing-room-only, crawling with uniformed officials. NYPD, SEC . . . clusters of initials that made my head swim.

The office itself had been trashed. Desk drawers pulled completely out, contents emptied, overturned on the ground amidst sheets and sheets of paper. File folders splayed across every available surface. A telltale wire wastebasket with the remains of something that had been shredded. Probably recently.

"What's going on?" I asked, despite the voice inside my head telling me *exactly* what was going on. What I should have known would be coming, eventually. If I'd bothered to pay attention to the signs. To recognize even my own family's fallibility.

"Don't say a word." It was Roger Glassman, Daddy's chief attorney. So, he was here. And he was telling Daddy to stay silent—even with me, his own daughter.

No wonder the folks at Barneys thought my father and his lawyers would be "otherwise occupied."

No wonder my credit cards were declined.

Yes, I'd missed a news flash. Or seven. And a few hundred obvious signs.

For years, there'd been whispers of Daddy and some possibly shady business dealings. I never listened, of course. Weren't *all* successful businessmen accused of being cheats and frauds at one point or another? It was the cost of success: a target on your back. *"Most kings get their heads cut off."* And here, at last, was Daddy's moment at the guillotine. And all his friends and colleagues here, gruesomely, to see him off. Delighting in his downfall. Grateful they'd dodged the bullet themselves this time.

"Ms. Veronica Lodge?" one of the officers approached me.

I glanced at Glassman, who gave me a nod. "Yes."

"Your father's facing some very serious charges. We have a warrant to search the premises, and we expect we'll be taking him under arrest when we're through." His eyes were kinder than I might have expected, like he was sorry to have to be dragging me into this. "You might want to wait in the hallway, or another room, while we finish up."

"Listen to him, *M'hija,*" Mom said. Her worry lines had deepened into fault lines across her forehead.

"Mom—"

"Listen to him," she repeated, softer, but still firmly this time.

I wanted to be brave, strong, and proud—to be the kind of person who could face the crowd waiting, hovering like vultures, in the living room. But I guess I'm not that person at heart—not when push truly comes to shove. Because when I left the room, I fled immediately to what I imagined to be the safety and privacy of my own bedroom.

Except, the room wasn't private. In fact, it wasn't empty at all. My friends had gathered there: Annie, Cam, Nick . . . My eyes welled up and my heart soared with gratitude. Thank god for friends, or this moment would be completely intolerable.

"You guys," I said, breathless, "it's insane in there. They're searching all of Daddy's files, looking for . . . I don't even know what! They say"—I paused to keep a tear from escaping—"they're going to arrest him."

I flopped down on the four-poster bed. Really, I wanted to curl into a ball, to have my mother pull the covers over me and rub my back, to reassure me that this would all be okay, despite every indication that that was not how it was going to be at all. "Thank you," I said soulfully, "for being here. For not leaving. For sticking by me." I swallowed. "You really are true friends."

There was a long pause. As close as we were, these people weren't used to such earnest displays from Veronica Lodge, I knew. Maybe I'd been too raw, too real?

But then, it started: first, a low chuckle, coming from Nick St. Clair himself, who'd only just this morning professed undying love for me. Then Annie chimed in, a shrieking laugh that sounded like a hyena, or some other wild animal. Last but not least was Cam, the one girl I'd thought I was closest to—surely my best friend, after Katie—who doubled over, laughing so hard she had to wipe tears from the corners of her eyes.

I sat up very straight on the bed. "What's going on?" Even though, truth be told, I knew. I more than knew.

"You thought we came because we're your friends, Ronnie?" Cam asked, sending herself into another spasm of hysteria. *"Please."*

"You knew this was coming." It wasn't a question.

"Girl, *everyone* knew this was coming. Our parents have been talking about it for weeks. I guess yours tried to keep it from you. And succeeded." Cam sounded so goddamn pleased with herself.

"The only reason we came tonight was because we wanted front row seats to the carnage," Nick said.

Was my head spinning, or the room? Sure, Daddy played hardball, and yes, he had his enemies, but this? The people I thought were my friends were here literally to laugh at my pain? "What about . . . what was all that stuff from this morning, Nick?" I asked, my stomach turning just remembering it.

"Oh, yeah!" His eyes brightened. "That was just a little something extra we cooked up, to make this moment really"—he made a "chef's kiss" motion—"stick."

"You're sick," I told him. "No wonder I always found you so utterly resistible."

"Oh, shut it, Ronnie," Annie said. "You weren't into Nick because you were too busy hooking up with any guy any of us ever mentioned we might be into. Because you're *such a good friend*."

I stared at her, my breath coming fast. "Like it's my fault that no guy would take Payless if they could have Prada instead? Take a long, hard look in the mirror—"

"Take a long, hard look into your *soul*, *Ronniekins*," Cam snapped. "Oh, no, wait—you haven't got one! Like father, like daughter."

Annie got in my face, so close I could smell the orange Tic Tacs she must've been sucking on while she waited for me to come home. "Since the freaking first grade, you've been terrorizing our school. You think you're untouchable, that we fall in line because we worship you so much. Meanwhile, everyone *hates* you, Ronnie. You deserve everything coming to you. Your dad is the worst con artist sleazebag since Bernie Madoff, and he's going down. And there's no effing way you or your mother are going to come out unscathed."

Cam moved in next to her. "*Karma's a bitch, Veronica*," she sang low. "But not as bad as you."

The three of them walked out together, holding hands like kids on a playground, still laughing.

∿∿∿

As promised, they took Daddy away that night. By then, the guests had finally been ushered out—though we had to call a reluctant Christopher to take care of clearing the space. He looked sorry for us, for what Mom and I were being dragged through.

But not that sorry.

Once the apartment was empty, Mom finally took off her heels. Still in her party couture, she collapsed onto the parlor settee with a generous glass of wine in hand. She shook some small white pills from a tiny box she pulled from a pocket and gulped them down with the alcohol. Even I knew that wasn't a great sign.

Finally, I had my moment to curl up in her lap. She stroked my hair, and didn't once complain that I was definitely staining her white dress with my cheek highlighter. To say that was the least of our problems was . . . the height of understatement.

"When will he be back?" I asked, my voice wobbly.

"I don't know, *M'hija,*" Mom admitted. "The people who've got him have wanted him for a long time."

"But . . . he's innocent, right? He has to be. What Cam was saying . . . it can't be true."

She was silent. I could feel her chest rise and fall with her breath. She smelled like freesia and tuberose, her favorite perfume. I'd never be able to associate that scent with feeling safe again, would I?

"What now?" I asked.

"Well," she said slowly, "the assets are seized, at least temporarily. Which means our budget is . . . severely compromised."

"We're broke."

"Not quite. Not by most people's standards. But we're going to have to make some . . . lifestyle changes."

I sat up, worried. "Such as?"

"Well, for starters, this apartment. The overhead is unbelievable. They're strict about subletting here, but I can probably get a special dispensation. Believe it or not, I still have a friend or two on the board."

"Sublet? Then, where will we go? Out to the Hamptons? To the lake house?" It wasn't ideal, but it also wasn't the very worst way to spend the summer, after all.

But Mom shook her head at that. "I wish we could, *M'hija*. But those are assets. And we won't have access to them until your father is free."

"Proven innocent."

"Free," she insisted, refusing to give any ground. "One way or another."

"So, where are we going to go?" We had family, of course, lots of extended family, but I doubted Mom wanted to go slinking back to them in our darkest hour. It was a matter of pride.

"Well," Mom said, putting down her wineglass. "Actually,

I've already made arrangements. I thought it was important to be prepared."

"You knew! You knew this was coming and you hid it from me."

"I was trying to protect you," she said. "I was worried, but I was holding out hope that everything would be fine. That it wouldn't come to this."

"I guess I can understand why you'd do that," I said, interlacing my fingers through hers. "So, these arrangements?"

"Do you remember the town I grew up in?"

"Uh, only bits and pieces. That tiny little two-bit Norman Rockwell/*Brigadoon* mashup of . . . wait . . . maple syrup, milk shakes, and doo-wop music, right?"

She laughed. "Sort of. There's more to it than that."

"Um, no offense, but it doesn't sound like there's that much more."

"It's not so bad," she assured me. "You'll see."

"Upstate, right? River Vale?"

"Yes, off the Metro North. River*dale*."

"Right, okay," I groaned, trying to be good-natured. It was hard. "I guess I'll be sure to pack my poodle skirts and bobby socks."

Mom squeezed me tight. "Pack them quickly, *M'hija*," she said. "We leave tomorrow."

Hey, readers—who here remembers Veronica Lodge, the heiress apparent to Wolf of Wall Street Hiram Lodge of Lodge Industries? Not ringing any bells? The ins and outs of the world of finance not exactly your typical preferred flavor of gossip?

We promise: You know Ronnie. You've seen her air-kissing Rihanna in photos from last year's Met Gala. And she's collaborating with the Olsen twins on a series of vegan leather handbags, too, we hear.

For the NYC social elite, an invite to the Lodge's Fourth of July bash is the hot ticket. We were all set to give you the complete 411. But this year, things got a touch . . . shall we say, overheated?

Poor little rich girl came home to her own fete only to find the Feds carting Daddy away. If you're feeling up for a dose of schadenfreude, you can read the full arrest report **here**. Lodge Industries has yet to release a statement at this time.

All we can say is this: Where there's smoke, there's fire. And this is one diva whose life's gone up in flames.

–Cleo T. for *Hello Giggles*

CHAPTER TWENTY

ARCHIE

For a self-proclaimed uncomplicated guy, I had a lot of thoughts churning around in my head while I packed a backpack to meet up with Geraldine: dishonesties between Dad and me, distance between Jug and me, the fact that now that I'd discovered music, I was pulling away from the Bulldogs and everything that used to define me in the first place.

The fact that I was involved with my music teacher and couldn't tell a soul about it.

"Pack light," she'd instructed, when we first talked about the overnight campout. "We won't need much." And I was sure she was right, but I was so keyed up I barely even noticed what I was throwing into the bag: a T-shirt, some clean socks. A flashlight, a water bottle. I wasn't Dilton Doiley, I didn't need some kind of survivalist kit.

Honestly, I was missing Betty.

I wouldn't have been able to tell her about Geraldine—I knew she wouldn't approve; Betty was such a good girl she'd never be on board with anyone breaking the rules that way. But I *wanted* to tell her. Or, I don't know, just to talk to her about anything. About nothing at all. Shoot the breeze like we used to all the time, before she left for LA.

Instinctively, I looked toward her bedroom window. The light was on, which threw me off. A blond head was looking through the dresser, opening and closing the drawers and shaking her head. For a second I thought I was seeing things. But then I realized: wrong blond. It was Polly, not Betty, rooting around.

I rapped on my window, our old symbol for getting each other's attention, long before either of us had phones. Polly looked up, even though it had been mine and Betty's thing, of course. She slid the window open and gestured for me to do the same.

"What's up?" I asked.

She glanced over her shoulder furtively, like she didn't want to be heard by someone in the house. "Have you spoken to Betty recently?"

I shook my head. "Nah, we really haven't talked since she left for LA." It was the second time today I'd admitted as much, and it still hit me like a gut punch. "You?"

"I've been trying to reach her all day," she said, and for a second it looked like there was real panic in her eyes. "I, uh . . . well, I was going to leave her a note, but I don't want—you know, Mom searches our stuff—"

"Leave her a note? About what?" Polly was being weird enough to get me a little worried.

A look crossed her face, like she was considering something, changing her mind. "Never mind, whatever. It's fine," she said. "I'll, um, keep trying her."

"You sure?" Why did we all have so many secrets? And what was it going to cost us to keep them so tight to ourselves?

"Yeah. Just . . . well, if you talk to her, or when you do— let her know I was trying to reach her?"

"Chances are you'll end up getting in touch with her way before I do," I said. But she seemed so—I don't know, sad, and scared for some reason. I added, "But yeah, of course."

"Great." She sighed and her forehead relaxed. Whatever was going on, I'd managed to say the right thing.

And then, from down the street, I heard it: the three short honks that meant Geraldine was waiting for me, on a shadowy stretch where Dad wouldn't spot me.

It was time to go.

⋀⋀⋀

Geraldine knew a clearing that wasn't too far from Striker's Cove, but was completely secluded. She said a ring of elm trees had grown just beyond the riverbank that made a secret hideaway of their own. It wasn't hard to find our way down there, even in the dark. We kept our arms wrapped around each other's waists.

"How did the trees grow in this pattern?" I asked. "It's crazy. Like something out of a horror movie."

"Where's your sense of romance?" Geraldine asked. "Nature made us our very own tree house. Literally."

She unrolled some pads and lay a blanket across them. We debated pitching a tent, but decided we didn't need it. It was nice to be able to lie back and look up at the tree branches crisscrossing the sky. Stars peeked through in irregular bursts.

"It's beautiful here," Geraldine said, laying her head on my chest.

"It is. It makes me want to write a song." Cliché, maybe, or lame, but true.

"I brought my guitar," she said. "But I don't think we should play it if we're trying to lay low. Sound carries, and you were saying you think the Adventure Scouts are nearby."

"No, you're right." I turned to one side so we were facing each other and wound my fingers through her hair. "It's okay."

"I'm sure we can find other ways to pass the time," she said.

After that, there wasn't much talking.

∼∼∼

I don't know how late we stayed up, completely caught up in each other. There were stars against the sky, and then the darkness began to drain. At some point, we must've fallen asleep. When I woke, I realized two things with a start:

First, that there were five missed calls on my phone. One was from Reggie, going off about Bulldog loyalty. The rest, though—they were all from Jughead. *Oh no.* Not only had I told my dad I'd be hanging with Jughead, but I'd told *Jughead* that, too.

A pit formed in my stomach. I was an awful friend.

Then the second realization came, fast and clear and searingly certain. I sat up, panicked, and realized that Geraldine was doing the same.

We both put it together at the same time, what it was that woke us up. It wasn't the breaking daylight, or Dilton Doiley's bugle revelry. It was a different sound: unmistakable, and un-ignorable. It was a sound I'd never forget.

A gunshot.

EPILOGUE

JUGHEAD

Our story is about a town, a small town. And the people who live in that town, who intersect each other's paths like wayward pinballs.

From a distance, it presents itself like so many other small towns all over the world: Safe. Decent. Innocent.

Get closer, though, and you start seeing the shadows underneath.

Riverdale: the town with pep! But every small town has its secrets.

One story of Riverdale—of so many of us in Riverdale—came to a head the night before the Fourth of July, events converging into cataclysmic inflection points from which we'd never recover. Betty, Archie, Veronica, and me; we were all, unwittingly, at a tipping point.

For us, it felt like an end.

But for one person in particular, it was the end. The real, permanent end.

One person we'd least expect to meet such a fate.

And so, like all good narratives, our story—Riverdale's story, the myriad tentacles that pulled us all into and out of one another's orbit seemingly without our own awareness, much less volition—our story became circular. Our endings led to a new story, a new beginning.

This *story begins with what the Blossom twins did on the Fourth of July.*

Just after dawn, Jason and Cheryl drove out to Sweetwater River for an early morning boat ride, as was their custom.

The next thing we know for certain is that Dilton Doiley, who was leading Riverdale's Adventure Scout Troop on a bird-watching expedition, came upon Cheryl by the river's edge. She was sopping wet, sobbing, calling for Jason. But he was gone. He'd fallen out of the boat, she explained, trying to retrieve her lost glove. The theory was that he'd panicked and drowned.

Riverdale police dragged Sweetwater River for Jason's body, but never found it.

So a week later, the Blossom family buried an empty casket, and Jason's death was ruled an accident.

Of course, Jason was captain of every sports team at Riverdale High, including water polo. And during summer vacations, he worked as a lifeguard at the country club. Which made one wonder about an accidental drowning. But nobody asked too many questions; the Blossoms were like poison roses in the garden of Riverdale, and no one wanted to get pricked by those venomous thorns.

The Fourth of July Tragedy would soon become just another urban legend—a cautionary tale we would regurgitate endlessly.

Until, or unless, some new revealing detail came to light.

Every small town has its secrets. And so did the four of us. We thought we'd locked them in our own private mental vaults, boxed them up, and put them behind us. Little did we know that was impossible to do.

Soon Veronica herself would descend on Riverdale, opening up a new mystery, a new set of legends, speculations, and whispered stories.

There is an idea of Riverdale: of what kind of town it is, of what sort of families live there. A notion that it exists unchanged and unchanging, as if frozen in a time capsule. But that's only one aspect of it, and only on the surface.

The truth is, if you really *want to understand Riverdale and what kind of place it is, I have to tell you about the shadows. The town* beneath *the town.*

I have to tell you everything. We all do. We have to come clean. It's time.

ABOUT THE AUTHOR

Micol Ostow has written over fifty works for readers of all ages, including projects based on properties like *Buffy the Vampire Slayer, Charmed*, and most recently, *Mean Girls: A Novel*. As a child she drew her own Archie comics panels, and in her former life as an editor she published the *Betty & Veronica Mad Libs* game. She lives in Brooklyn with her husband and two daughters, who are also way too pop culture–obsessed. Visit her online at micolostow.com.